Alaskan Holiday

A novel by Larry Charrier

Larry Charrier (signature)

GREAT WAVE
Publishing

Library of Congress Catalog Card Number: 98-71584

ISBN 0-9640637-2-7

Cover Design by Terri Metcalf

Great Wave Publishing
P.O. Box 23139
Ketchikan, AK
99901

This Book is dedicated to Erik and Charlotte.

Thanks to Quenn, Randy, Karen, Gretchen, and Diane for their help and encouragement.

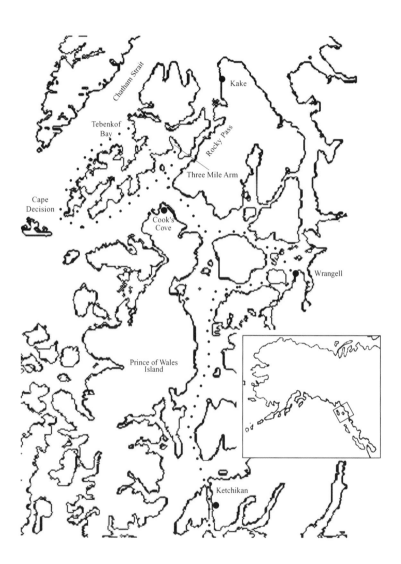

Chatham Strait

Kake

Tebenkof
Bay

Rocky Pass

Three Mile Arm

Cape
Decision

Cook's
Cove

Wrangell

Prince of Wales
Island

Ketchikan

Chapter One

At the sound of the shot, the bear whirled, scrambled over a jumble of drift logs, and disappeared into the thick coastal forest. He'd given no indication of having been hit, but from where I crouched less than a hundred yards away I'd heard the sickening thud as the bullet struck flesh.

I'd been observing the young black bear for several minutes when suddenly a hunter had appeared from around a point on the opposite end of the beach. He sat down, took careful aim, and fired. While not aiming directly at me, the shot had been close enough to my general direction that I'd instinctively ducked behind a large spruce log, tossed high on the shore by some violent storm years ago.

Peering cautiously over the log, my heart racing from this sudden shattering of the peaceful scene I'd beheld just seconds ago, I wondered what to do next. True, I'd found the shooting of the bear right in front of me shocking, but after all, I rationalized, there's plenty of black bears in Southeast Alaska. The hunting season might be open now, I wasn't sure. Since it obviously hadn't been a trophy-sized animal this was probably just a case of a guy needing some meat and legally going about getting it. Nothing I should get worked up over.

I just about decided to stand up and reveal myself, maybe even offer to help the guy recover the bear and drag it back to the beach. He must have a boat somewhere nearby, though I hadn't seen it. But something held me back. I focused my binoculars on the shooter. A young man dressed in blue jeans and a gray sweat shirt, with long brown hair hanging below a dark cap, he was leaning against a boulder smoking a cigarette. His scope-sighted rifle was propped up beside him. He looked awfully casual.

After finishing the cigarette he picked up his rifle, chambered a fresh round and carefully pocketed the empty cartridge. He'd made no attempt of a second shot at the fleeing bear. After a final long look around he walked directly to where the bear had been and followed its path into the woods.

I was certain he was unaware of my presence, concealed as I was behind the log. I hadn't proceeded any further down the beach, so had left no foot prints, and my sailboat lay anchored in a snug cove behind me, separated by a narrow isthmus of timbered land, and out of sight.

Well, I didn't really feel like helping some guy fool with a dead or wounded bear, especially a wounded one since I was unarmed. I quietly began to retrace my steps towards the boat, but again had second thoughts. What if he ran into trouble with a wounded bear? Selecting a position just inside the dark woods where I was unlikely to be detected but still had a good view of the beach, I sat down and leaned against an old hemlock snag. I'd just wait here to determine the outcome of this little drama.

Scarcely ten minutes had passed when the hunter reappeared on the beach, heading back the way he'd come. I hadn't heard any more shots so either the bear was dead or he'd given up on tracking it. His rifle was slung over his shoulder and, through the binoculars, I could see what appeared to be a small plastic bag containing something red and bloody dangling from his right hand.

Uh huh, I thought. He's gutted out the dead bear, and done a quick job of it too. Now he's taking the liver with him on the way to get his boat. He'll be back in a few minutes for the rest of the carcass.

He'd no sooner passed from sight, when a pair of ravens flew over and began circling and calling excitedly over what I assumed was the dead bear. Soon two more appeared. I sat watching the birds swoop and dive, wondering how soon one of them would work up the nerve to land and sample their newfound banquet, when I heard an outboard motor start up in the distance.

The engine idled smoothly then accelerated into the high-pitched whine of a powerful outboard motor. I expected to see a boat round the point at any moment, but instead the sound seemed to grow dimmer. Soon it faded away altogether. It puzzled me at first, but then I reasoned he must have a friend nearby. He'd go pick him up and together they'd return for the bear.

I stood up. My butt was wet from the damp moss. It was getting late and I was getting hungry. I hurried back towards my boat anticipating the fresh halibut fillet I had waiting for my dinner. Following an old bear trail across the narrow neck of land, wading through blueberry bushes, skirting huge moss-draped windfalls among the standing timber, and finally breaking through a shoreside tangle of small alders, I arrived at the cove where my boat was anchored. I paused, as I always did, to admire my vessel.

Lapstrake construction, with a lively sheer, the 22-foot double-ended sloop looked good to me. For a man my age, I thought, I took an inordinate amount of satisfaction in having built her. I'd done a lot of boat work over the past thirty years but this was the first one I'd actually built from start to finish. And the first sailboat I'd ever been on.

The dinghy lay on some logs, above the high tide-line where I'd left it. Hoisting all twenty-eight pounds of it I hooked one gunwale on my right shoulder and headed for the water. It was an odd little craft but suited my purposes well enough. I'd built this one too, but unlike my sailboat, I'd actually designed my "ding-yak", as I called it.

Built of thin plywood and epoxy, it was 11 1/2 feet long by 30 inches wide and propelled by a kayaker's double bladed paddle. Unlike a kayak, it was mostly open, but the unique feature was that the ends unhooked and stowed in the center section. I could fold the whole thing into a 48-inch by 30-inch box and lash it down on my foredeck, eliminating the hassle of towing a dinghy.

I managed to get the thing into the water and myself into it, then paddle out to the sailboat and climb aboard without getting wet. No mean feat for a 50-year-old, 200-pound man, and something I didn't take for granted, though I was getting better at using it. I'd had lots of practice lately.

After my dinner of fried halibut and boiled potatoes I thought about the bear shooting. Something about it troubled me. Maybe it was the man's apparent total casualness. Also I couldn't remember ever hearing of anyone eating bear liver. In fact I vaguely recalled reading somewhere that polar bear's liver was so high in some vitamins that it was actually poisonous to humans.

No sounds of outboard motors disturbed the near silence of the cove that evening. I wasn't certain I would've heard one approach the beach where the bear had been anyway. It was a distance away, and the still summer evening brought out the mosquitoes and 'no-see-ums', which kept me inside the tiny cabin of the sailboat.

An odd little chirping call worked its way into my

consciousness early the next morning as I wavered between wakefulness and sleep. The sound was vaguely familiar, but I couldn't place it. I swung my legs off the bunk and got my pants part way on. Then, hunched over in an awkward position, shuffled a couple of steps aft, slid open the hatch and straightened up. With head and shoulders now protruding above the hatch opening, I zippered and buttoned my pants and took in the early morning scene.

A light mist rose from the still waters of the cove and swirled among the dark, overhanging evergreens. A disturbance in the water caught my eye and I watched as three river otters swam ashore and disappeared among the boulders in an odd, humping gait. So that was the sound. Now I remembered. Strange that these animals made such a little, birdlike call.

Over a cup of black tea, liberally laced with canned milk, I thought about the coming day's plan. Not that I really needed much of one. I'd been on the boat for over two months now, slowly heading north from Puget Sound when the winds and tides were favorable, checking out all the places I'd rushed past over the years in my bigger and faster fishing boats, intent on earning a season's income.

The breeze out in the channel was in the right direction. I was tempted to pull the anchor and get an early start, but that business with the bear troubled me. I decided to take another look. The ding-yak was still in the water lashed alongside the sailboat. I gingerly lowered myself in. Both the bow and stern lines led to a point amidships, allowing me to untie them while seated in the center of the small, tippy boat. I cast off and paddled towards shore.

Unlike yesterday though, I didn't land at the nearest available place, but, keeping outside the kelpline, just offshore, paddled a half mile out around the rocky point and then directly to the large, leaning spruce tree that marked that spot where the bear had disappeared into the forest. I beached there.

Looking closely, I detected dried blood on the logs where the bear had crossed. I followed the faint trail left by the bleeding bear and the man. Certainly no dead bear had been dragged back along here and I saw no indication that anyone had returned to the area. It gave me a spooky feeling and I wished I had brought along my old Marlin 30-30 that was on the boat. I didn't want to go back for it though, so continued on.

Fifty yards in, I came upon the dead bear. He'd died from a well placed shot, broadside through the lungs, which had given him just enough time for one last, quick burst of energy to run this far and keel over. Probably he was dead by the time the shooter had taken two drags on his cigarette. I had a feeling the shooter had known this, but for the life of me, I couldn't figure out the rest of it.

A small incision had been made on the bear's stomach and some of his guts had spilled out. But that was all. I got a stick and poked at his innards and couldn't see that anything major was missing. How strange! Maybe the guy started to dress out the animal and cut himself and went for first aid. He didn't seem like he had a problem though, the way he walked down the beach. And why the bloody bag? The whole thing was a puzzle.

No predators or scavengers had bothered the carcass, apparently not even the curious ravens. I had a good pocket knife and considered removing a few steaks, but, in the end, decided against it. I didn't want anything to do with it. I hurried back to the ding-yak and paddled to the sailboat, anxious to get out of there.

Unfortunately, by the time I got everything stowed away and the anchor up the wind had quit and a light rain set in. Reluctantly I started my little five horsepower Honda outboard and motored out the bay.

So far on the trip I'd done as little motoring as possible. I prided myself in having used only twenty-five gallons of gas in eight hundred miles. Leaving Puget Sound in late April had allowed me plenty of time to catch some southeast winds before the predominantly westerly winds of summer began. Even with my limited sailing experience, I realized that compared to sailing downwind, tacking up a narrow channel into the wind was a hard way to get somewhere.

Now I had no wind. Often when in a pleasant location I'd wait days for favorable conditions, but I didn't feel like staying here. So, droning along the channel at four knots, hunched over in my rain gear in the open cockpit with one hand draped over the tiller, I wondered for perhaps the hundredth time on this trip, what I was doing screwin' around up here in this little sailboat.

Oh, I knew that any armchair psychologist would quickly label it as a case of "mid-life crisis" and let it go at that. But it felt like more than that to me. True, my family life was in upheaval. Last year my wife had moved to Seattle, rented an apartment, gotten a job and enrolled in college; in short, started a new life of her own. Our only child, a daughter, was in college, off in Missoula, Montana. I was left alone at our home on the Olympic Peninsula, puttering around my shop, building this boat.

I'd spent thirty years commercial fishing, going through a succession of boats, working my way up to my present 47-footer, each one decked out with better equipment and more and more electronics. The seasons grew shorter and shorter over the years, and more competitive and frantic as the fleet grew more efficient and the number of fish remained the same. I felt caught up in a rat race and wanted a break.

I wanted to get my eyes off the radar screen and fish-finding sonar, and back on the scenery. Wanted to take the time to explore, and enjoy the sunsets. It sounded corny, but I wanted to feel closer to nature, to travel on the water without a diesel engine thundering in my ears and stinking up the air. I wanted to recapture at least some of the beauty and awe and magic I'd felt on my first seasons in Alaska.

And to some extent I'd been successful. Watching the yellow cedar shavings curl from my hand and pile up on the floor as I shaped a piece of wood, and watching the boat grow plank by plank into a creation of grace and beauty, had been eminently satisfying. Learning to sail, gliding with an evening breeze along a wild shoreline, the sails barely drawing, and coasting into a secluded anchorage without a sound, or reefed down on a beam reach in a stout westerly all the way across Queen Charlotte Sound, had all been exciting, and humbling too. Yet, like most things, these feelings had been transitory and at times like now, I wondered.

Throughout the day I steered a course up Stikine Channel, for the town of Wrangell, Alaska. By late afternoon the rain turned to scattered showers and a nice southwest breeze sprang up. From my seat in the cockpit, I slacked the line to the roller furling, then hauled in on my jib sheet. The jib sail unrolled smoothly, like pulling down a window shade, and I was sailing.

I shut off the outboard and tipped it up so the lower unit wouldn't be dragging through the water, causing resistance. The mainsail halyard led aft through a block, and, without leaving the cockpit, I hoisted the main. Another adjustment on the jib and I leaned back and relaxed. Now this was more like it, sailing on a broad reach, running free before the wind towards my destination.

A stronger gust hit. The boat heeled slightly and picked up speed, but my hand remained relaxed on the tiller. This was no white knuckle, high speed, fin keeled, racing sailboat, but a moderately rigged, more traditional cruising boat. A classic design with a relatively shallow full-length keel containing a thousand pounds of lead ballast kept her fairly stiff and tracking well. To me, she handled beautifully, whether barely making way in the lightest of breezes, or slicing through the waves at hull speed with little commotion.

The only change I'd made from the original design was adding the roller furling on the jib. To some it may have seemed extravagant on such a small boat. But at my age I had no interest in balancing on a pitching foredeck, trying to handle a flapping sail. The device was so simple and worked so well that I found myself gloating every time I used it.

I approached Wrangell in the long, summertime twilight. The town lies some seventy-five miles east of the outer coast where I'd normally fished. I hadn't been there for years, and didn't expect to see anyone I knew, which was one of the reasons I'd decided to stop in there. I didn't feel like explaining what I was doing.

Just off the breakwater of the small boat harbor I rolled up the jib, then pushed the tiller over and hove to. I clipped the aft end of the boom to the backstay so it wouldn't swing around, then lowered the main and lashed it to the boom. I might have sailed in had I known exactly where I'd tie up. But, not remembering the layout of the harbor, I chose the more prudent course of using the engine.

The boat harbor was fairly quiet, as most of the commercial fishermen were off chasing salmon somewhere in the vast reaches of southeast Alaska. Eyeing the transient float, I approached slowly. Along most of its length boats were rafted up two or three deep, a collection of live aboards, cruisers, and old fish boats. There was one empty space, but I hesitated to use it; too much chance someone would raft up beside me during the night and wake me up. I chose a troller that, judging by its state of neglect, didn't look like it would be leaving anytime soon, and tied up alongside, third boat out from the float.

I decided to stretch my legs and take a walk uptown. From the top of the ramp I noticed a boat that I recognized being unloaded at the fish dock. Most trollers didn't run this far in from the grounds to sell their catch, as there were other buyers closer, but I knew the owner of this boat lived here, and had probably come in for that reason. I hadn't really wanted to run into anyone I knew, but I couldn't help myself. I wanted to see how he'd done. Like a moth to a hundred watt bulb, I was drawn to the unloading boat.

He'd done well. Several loads of bright, twenty and thirty pound king salmon were hoisted from his hold as I looked on, fighting back pangs of envy, thinking maybe I should've been out there too. Just as I turned to leave, Wally came out the office door and caught me. He looked at me, glanced around the harbor, then looked back. "Dave, what are you doing here? Where's your boat?"

"Oh, it's tied up at the dock back in Washington."

"Yeah, I didn't see you out on the grounds, or hear you on the radio. What'd ya do, quit?"

I shrugged. "I don't know. Takin' a break from the yearly grind anyway."

"I don't blame ya. You got time for a quick one?"

"Sure, I'm not goin' anywhere."

He hollered down to his deck hand to be sure to clean the hold good and fill the bins with three tons of new ice. "We'll be leavin' in the morning," he said. "Make sure you're aboard."

I followed him over to his pickup and we rattled a couple of blocks to the nearest tavern. Wally didn't say anything on the way. He had that dazed, slightly disoriented look of someone who's just gotten off a boat after a hard trip and was trying to remember all the things he needed to do in the next few hours before he left again.

I could almost read his mind: "Let's see, already got ice. Fuel up in the morning. Change oil? Will the deckhand be there? Sober? What about that noise in the reverse gear? Have to check that out. Get groceries in the morning. Wife can help with that. Whoops, don't be too late for dinner. A shower sure is gonna feel good, and a night's sleep. Wonder which way I should head tomorrow? Last year the cohos really hit off Yakobi Island. It's a long run though."

Wally took a long first drink of his beer and let out a sigh. "Yeah, I don't blame ya," he repeated. "We just had a six day king salmon season. Six days! Christ, can you believe it? It gets shorter every year. It wasn't that long ago we fished 'em from April to October."

"Yeah, I know. But it looks like you got your share anyway." I knew better than to ask where he'd caught them.

"Sure. We did OK. Lucked out and were on the fish. But we could've just as easily missed 'em. Hell! It's more like a crap shoot now than a fishing season. One wrong move or a breakdown and you're outa luck, no time for a second chance."

"Tell me about it," I said. "Two years ago my alternator went out on the second day of king season, and my spare turned out to be the wrong one."

"All right," he grinned. "I guess I don't have to cry in my beer to you."

"Nope." I took a drink. "So you decided to run your fish all the way into town, huh?"

"Yeah. I got a deal worked out here. I get a better price if I bring 'em in. It's about a toss up though, cuz I'm gonna miss at least two days coho fishing now."

"Were they showin' up pretty good where you were?"

"No. It's still early for there. That's one reason I didn't mind runnin' in." He looked at his watch, then drained his beer. "Well, I gotta get goin'. I told the old lady I'd be home for dinner, and I gotta take care of some stuff yet tonight."

"OK." I watched him get up. Lookin' a little stiff like me, I noticed. "Oh, by the way," I said, "Have you seen Mac around this year, or heard anything of him?"

Wally thought for a second. "No, I haven't seen him. And he never talks on the radio unless he has to, but I think I heard some rumor this spring that he's holed up in his old floathouse up in Three Mile Arm."

"That's not too hard to believe, is it?"

"I suppose not." He gave his head a little shake as he walked towards the door.

Well, that hadn't been too bad. Wally had been so hurried and preoccupied he hadn't asked what I was doing. I'd been saved the bother and potential embarrassment of trying to explain. The bar had a kitchen of sorts, and since I was already there and hungry, I ordered a cheeseburger and another beer.

The burger was gone and my glass nearly empty when I found myself studying someone seated alone across the room. Something seemed vaguely familiar about him. He lit a cigarette and I suddenly got the connection. Same black cap and long hair. He reminded me of the guy who had shot the bear, just yesterday. Walking past him on the way to the restroom, I glanced furtively at his outline from different angles. Seemed like him all right. I wondered if I should question him. No bandages showed on his hands, so I reasoned he couldn't have injured himself enough to warrant leaving the animal. If he had been the one, and I was pretty sure he was, he could easily deny it and that would be the end of it. I wasn't prepared to call him a liar.

Heading back to the bar, I noticed he was being joined by a man who had just come in. I ordered another beer and moved to a closer table. Close enough, I hoped, to overhear their conversation, but not seem too intrusive. Black cap looked at me and scowled when I sat down, but the other man ignored my presence. Of the two young men, he was the more respectable looking. His carefully combed blonde hair, clean shaven face and expensive looking lightweight wool jacket contrasted sharply with black cap's overall scruffy and unkempt appearance.

I strained to catch their words, while trying to look totally uninterested. It wasn't easy. They had to talk fairly loud to hear themselves over the din of the jukebox, but it also effectively drowned out their conversation for me. The clean one seemed to do most of the talking, though I couldn't make out what he was saying. Then on a break between songs I heard black cap say, "There's gettin' to be a lot of people out and around this time of year."

"True," said the clean one, "but the market's here now. You'll just have to be..." He suddenly realized he didn't need to talk so loud, and, glancing over at me, lowered his voice. I continued to stare vacantly into space somewhere to the right of them.

After that the conversation seemed to lag. I assumed they were talking about some seafood market and was tired of trying to listen anyway. I walked down the hallway past the restrooms to a pay phone on the wall, just inside the back door.

Halfway through dialing my wife's number I hesitated. I wanted to talk to her, tell her where I was, and that I'd be heading back south soon. But it's late, I told myself. She's probably in bed. I shouldn't bother her. The truth of the matter, though, was that I was afraid to call at night. What if some man answered? Or I heard one in the background? I had no reason to believe she wasn't alone, but if someone was with her I didn't want to know about it.

As I stood there, with phone in hand, number half dialed, the clean one walked past me and out the back door. Through the window, I saw him climb into a newer model, four-wheel drive pickup. The dome light briefly revealed an older oriental man sitting in the passenger seat before they drove off.

I hung up the phone and walked back through the bar. Black cap was still sitting there nursing his drink. He watched me as I passed by, and I felt his eyes follow me out the front door. Oh well, what did I care? Maybe he did shoot a bear and leave it in the woods. I had enough problems of my own.

Chapter Two

After leaving the bar I went for a walk through Wrangell. For some reason thoughts of my wife quickly receded and I found myself dwelling on Wally's comments about my old friend Mac. I hadn't seen him for a few years now, but, of all the fisherman I knew up here, he was the one person I'd feel comfortable encountering while on my sailboat.

Although I knew many would disagree, I'd often considered him the sanest of the lot of us. Sure, he had his problems, and some people, I'm quite certain, would be quick to point out that love of alcohol and lack of ambition were two big ones. I held him in high regard nonetheless.

He was the genuine article, an old-timer, a real Alaskan Sourdough. Yet I knew I'd never see his photo on the cover of a magazine or book. He wasn't that noticeable, and probably wouldn't be considered a colorful enough character unless you got to know him well, which would take awhile.

Not that he wasn't well known by some. I'm sure most of the older trollers knew him, or at least knew of him. He could definitely catch salmon when he put his mind to it, which admittedly wasn't as often as it used to be. In the old days, when the seasons were longer and more fishing was done on inside waters instead of the open ocean like now, he had a reputation for bringing in nice loads of king salmon he'd caught in some obscure little hole when no one else could find any. Just when you got used to seeing him around somewhere, he had a habit of slipping away undetected. He might show up in a few days with a load of fish, or might not be seen again for months.

Unlike some experienced hands, Mac would occasionally share his knowledge. Over the years, whether repairing a breakdown or putting them on the fish, he helped out many a fisherman, novice and veteran alike, myself included.

Not that he would just lead anyone to a school of hungry fish. He liked his privacy, and if an area became too crowded, even if the fishing was good, he'd leave. He hardly ever talked on the radio, and his boat was painted a combination of green and gray that matched the shoreline, making it almost impossible to detect from a distance.

Most fisherman had running partners and they fished more or less together, or shared their fishing information in carefully coded radio conversations, lest they reveal a concentration of salmon to the rest of the fleet. Mac seemed to prefer traveling by himself though, and at times could be downright secretive about where he was going or had been. But then again, he might pass on a little advice to a beginner.

The first time I met him was down in Sea Otter Sound. It was my third year of trolling and first year all by myself. I felt like I was beginning to figure things out. The cohos hadn't come in yet, but there were just enough king salmon to keep me and a handful of other boats working the sound's numerous inlets and bays. One of them was Mac, on his boat the *Hazel Belle*.

We were fishing more or less the same area, or drag, as it was called, and occasionally would pass close by one another. He returned my wave, and I saw him land a few fish. I felt I was doing well and assumed we were catching a similar amount while he was there, but he always seemed to disappear around noon.

I wondered where he went. I knew it wasn't far since, like me, he appeared on the drag bright and early each morning. After three or four days of fishing near him in the mornings, I trolled further than normal up around the island in the direction he'd gone, and noticed him anchored in the back of a little bay on the opposite shore. Since I was fishing from dawn until late in the day, I quickly labeled him as somewhat of a piker, and chuckled to myself thinking of him missing out on the fairly good evening bite I'd gotten each day.

The fishing fell off, and, by chance, we both quit and headed for the fish buyer at Tokeen on the same afternoon. I was a little ahead, and had just finished unloading and cleaning my hold, and taking on ice, when Mac arrived.

I loitered at the fish buying scow, picking up a few groceries and supplies, feeling pleased with my recent catch. With sidelong glances and feigned indifference, I casually watched as Mac unloaded, wondering how many less fish he'd have than me since he'd only been fishing half days, and was in turn amazed, then dumbfounded, then disgusted, when the fish kept coming. He'd easily caught three times as many as I had.

As he tossed up the last salmon, a beauty weighing forty pounds, he looked up and caught me staring at him, probably looking like some slack-jawed idiot. My feelings of pride and well-being now totally shattered, I turned and sulked back to my boat.

I stayed tied to the dock in Tokeen that day, trying to simultaneously catch up on my rest and all the little chores that accumulated after several days of fishing, and wasn't particularly successful on either account. Later, after dinner, while out on deck working over my gear, I noticed

Mac on his boat nearby. He was sitting on his hatch cover, drinking a beer with a six-pack beside him. "Care for one?" He called out.

Walking over, I accepted the can and perched on the after bulwarks of his troller, mumbling my thanks.

"Don't mention it," he said. "By the way, my name's Mac."

Introductions over, I drank half my beer in silence. Mac sat watching me with a bemused half-smile on his stubble covered face. He was one of those guys whose age is hard to guess. I was in my early twenties at the time, and calculated he must be at least ten, or possibly twenty years my senior. A little smaller than me, he had close cropped, grayish-brown hair and no truly distinguishing features, other than upon a closer glance, a pair of light blue eyes with a very piercing look.

I turned fully towards him and, ignoring normal fisherman's protocol, bluntly asked what weighed so heavily on my mind. "So, how'd you catch so many more fish than me when you only fished half a day?" I blurted out.

He let out a little laugh. "What makes you so sure I only fished half a day?"

"Well, I saw you anchored up there around the island in the afternoon."

"True, I did anchor for awhile every afternoon and take a nap when things slowed down," he said with a grin. "But I went back out in the evening and had pretty good action off that reef on the other side, just before low water. The bait really collects there on the ebb sometimes."

"Oh," I said lamely. "I guess I've got a lot to learn."

"Don't we all," he laughed. He extracted two more cans from the six-pack and handed one to me. That was the beginning of our long lasting, if somewhat intermittent, friendship.

Arriving back at my sailboat, I hardly realized how I'd gotten there, so lost had I been in my thoughts and memories. I slept soundly and awoke with a new sense of purpose and direction for my trip. I'd cruise out to Mac's floathouse and see if he was still there.

If he was, I'd visit for awhile before I headed home. If he wasn't, I'd leave him a note and watch for him along my way down the west side of Prince of Wales Island. Then I'd round the southern tip of the island and cross into Canada and more or less retrace my route back to Washington while the good weather held out. My goal was to be well south of Queen Charlotte Sound by the first week of September.

I walked uptown and had a breakfast, stocked up on groceries, and called my wife. She wasn't home, or at least wasn't answering. I left a message on her machine explaining I'd check for mail at Cook's Cove before heading south.

I feel dumb talking to a machine and normally won't do it, preferring to just try again until I get the real person. But I knew I might not have a convenient chance to call again soon, and, even though our relationship was now strained, calling my wife whenever I was in port was a habit I couldn't easily shake, nor one I was sure I wanted to. I mumbled into the receiver that I hoped she was doing well, and hung up.

Wally's boat was gone when I got back to the dock. He'd had a good trip, and, even after all these years of fishing, I still felt twinges of envy about someone else landing fish when I didn't. The fact that I wasn't even fishing, but was off playing around on a sailboat instead, only seemed to confuse the issue. Oh well, I certainly didn't envy the pace and tensions he was caught up in.

There's something liberating about getting underway from town on a boat, leaving civilization behind. As the houses and buildings melt into the background, the concerns and complications of life seem to dwindle along with the noise and commotion. I never got the same uplift when getting underway from an anchorage, just hoisted the anchor and went about my business. But leaving the dock is different.

Today was no exception. The further I got from town, the better I felt. I didn't even mind that I was motoring in a flat calm instead of sailing. I amused myself for some time reflecting on how I gained a new perspective on things when on the water. Away from land I took on a more detached outlook to life's difficulties. My concerns were more simple and immediate: keep the boat going where it should, don't sink, catch fish. And now I didn't even have to worry about catching fish.

I realized I'd always been so caught up in what I was doing before, I'd never consciously thought these things through, even though I'd felt them. Now, instead of charging along on autopilot, tying up new leaders and thinking about where to fish, I cruised at a leisurely four knots, indulging in philosophical thoughts concerning the joys of getting underway.

Soon enough, my mind went full circle, and I had to laugh at my grandiose musings. True, it may have felt liberating to get away from town on occasion. But many times over the years I'd come back worn out, bruised, battered, and mentally and physically exhausted, wanting nothing more than to tie the boat to a sturdy dock, turn off the engine, and set foot on solid land.

As I cleared Vank Island, a breeze began to freshen and ripples formed on the otherwise smooth surface. A light southeaster, it was on my port quarter, so I rolled out the jib and hoisted the mainsail. The wind was erratic enough that I kept the engine running while taking advantage of the gentle gusts for an occasional increase in speed.

The breeze nearly died, then shifted as it flowed around the logged off hills of Zarembo Island, and now hit me on the port bow. Eventually it steadied to a nice blow of ten to fifteen knots. I turned off the engine and tipped it up, grateful for the silence.

Like most sailboats, mine has a slight weather helm, meaning if left untended it will slowly turn into the wind, so I lashed the tiller in place to keep her on a straight course. Stiff and cold, I slid the hatch open and stood in the companionway of the small trunk cabin, savoring a cup of hot tea.

Standing in the open hatchway, my elbows resting comfortably on the cabin roof, I let the boat sail herself while I took in the scenery. A tug and barge crossed a couple of miles in front of me, aiming for Wrangell Narrows, and a brilliant white cruise ship passed it on its way south. No other boat traffic was in sight. Clouds were thickening ahead, out over Sumner Strait and over the clearcut-speckled slopes of Mitkof Island. Behind, the tops of the tall jagged peaks on the mainland were already obscured. It looked like rain.

I don't relish the idea of sitting in the open cockpit, sailing in the rain, and normally would've begun looking for a snug anchorage. Now I had a destination, though, and the tide was with me, so I maintained course.

Off the mouth of Snow Pass the wind increased and the rain began. Donning full rain gear, I pressed on under reefed sails. By the time I reached Red Bay, ten miles further, where I would anchor for the night, it was whistling pretty good overhead, but I was in the lee of Prince of Wales Island and had smooth going.

I sailed in tight to the beach, rolled up the jib, swung

her up into the wind and doused the mainsail, then dropped the hook in four fathoms of water. Over thirty miles from Wrangell, I'd made what I considered to be a good day's passage. I was over half way to Three Mile Arm and Mac's floathouse. With luck, I'd make it in another day.

My luck didn't hold out. Instead of waking to the normal sounds of birds calling and the occasional splash of a jumping salmon, all I heard when I awoke was rain pounding on the cabin roof and wind blowing through nearby tree tops. The morning was so nasty looking, with gusty winds and sheets of rain, I stayed in my bunk as long as I could stand it, then spent half the day cooped up in my little cabin reading and eating. From time to time I'd peer out and look around, but even the wildlife, which is usually so evident in Alaskan bays in the summer, seemed to be hiding.

Conditions improved late that afternoon, and, anxious to get going, I quickly hoisted the anchor and set sail. I had a great sail, scudding down Sumner Strait on a reach under clearing skies. Since I'd gotten such a late start I planned on spending the night at the tiny community of Cook's Cove, popularly referred to as either Kook's Cove, no doubt due to the many eccentric individuals who had lived there over the years, or Crook's Cove, in regards to what some felt were exorbitant prices at the store and bar.

But the going was so good I decided against stopping and passed it by, two miles offshore, hoping to reach Mac's before dark. Rounding Point Barrie, I now had the wind almost directly astern and made excellent time for awhile, running before it. Unfortunately, the wind slackened, then quickly began to fade, soon to be followed by the remaining daylight.

Not wanting to attempt the rock strewn entrance to Three Mile Arm in the dark on a falling tide, plus not knowing the exact location of Mac's floathouse, I reluctantly anchored in a little bight off the north end of Conclusion Island. It was a poor anchorage. The wind had quit almost entirely now, though, and it wouldn't stay dark long this time of year. Anyway, I was used to sleeping lightly in dubious anchorages. I'd easily make Mac's tomorrow.

* * * * *

Mac stood on the deck of his floathouse looking at the top of his mast and trolling poles sticking out of the water beside him. The top of the rigging was all that was visible of his faithful old troller, which now rested on the bottom in twenty feet of water. And it had been there for two months. He shook his head disgustedly. What a mess!

Living alone in the Alaskan bush, he'd been in a lot of predicaments over the years, but this one was undoubtedly the dumbest. Right now, he felt about as low as the bottom of his boat's keel laying in the mud below him, and he kicked himself mentally for the hundredth time. If only he hadn't been so stupid.

True, he'd been tricked. Downright, flat out, cheated by that no good degenerate hanging out at Cook's Cove last winter. If he ever saw him again, which he was certain he wouldn't, the guy would definitely regret it. Anyone who would do that to another person up here in this country of few people wouldn't last long. He'd be run out, quick.

The guy had said he needed the money to fly out and Mac believed that. He'd need the cover of a larger population to hide his moral bankruptcy. Probably living a life of drinking, petty crime, and welfare fraud in some city about now, thought Mac. Then he grinned to himself. Stuck as he was, he still wouldn't trade places with anyone, especially that guy.

It had been a fairly clever trick, though Mac felt he should never have fallen for it. Of course if he hadn't gone on that binge up in Kake he wouldn't be in this situation now either, he reminded himself. "Oh, knock it off," he muttered out loud. He'd done what he could, with what he had, for now.

The faint drone of an engine interrupted Mac's thoughts, and he cocked his head, listening intently, hoping it would be an approaching boat. It turned out to be an airplane passing by unseen, somewhere in the distance. The fact that no boat had approached the floathouse for the last several months was an irony not lost on Mac. He'd picked his home place well.

Three Mile Arm, situated on the east side of Kuiu Island, off an almost dead end branch of Sumner Strait now that the Coast Guard had taken the buoys out of Rocky Pass and few people ventured through there, was an area seldom visited. Yet it wasn't so far away from civilization or surrounded by such large, potentially rough bodies of water that Mac couldn't get out to a town when he felt like it. Even in winter, given a day or two of good weather, he could reach Petersburg or Wrangell in his boat, or at least make the twenty mile run to Cook's Cove, where there was a store, a bar, a post office and a handful of people.

It's not that Mac disliked people, exactly. It was more like someone from down south had once explained to him how they felt about snow. They'd said snow was fine in its place, like up in the mountains, but it didn't need to come down to them. If they wanted to see snow, they'd prefer to drive to it. Mac felt somewhat the same about people. He didn't want to live among them. The couple of visitors he got each year were fine. Other than that, if he wanted to see people, he'd prefer to have to go to them.

But now, he was ready for someone to come by.

Mac had always prided himself on his patience and self reliance. Since he'd returned to his floathouse in his skiff this spring and discovered his boat sunk, then discovered his more disgusting problem of being out of gas, he'd unhurriedly and methodically gone about preparing to refloat and repair his boat. There was only so much he could do, however, before he needed some parts he didn't have. Since it was summer, he figured someone might come by who had some extra gas, but they hadn't, and now his patience, and the season, were both growing shorter.

He thought he could get the stuff he needed in Cook's Cove, but, with the way the tide raced and swirled through Sumner Strait, and the seas kicked up in such a hurry, he was extremely reluctant to attempt to row there. Maybe if he had a good seaworthy rowboat like a dory instead of a wide, flat, outboard, aluminum skiff he'd try it. But he didn't.

No, if someone didn't show up soon, even though it was farther, he'd row and drift with the tide the thirty some miles through Rocky Pass to Kake. There he'd get gas, but not, he was sure, the parts he needed. Then he'd run the skiff all the way back past Three Mile Arm and across to the Cove. Hopefully he'd get everything he needed there and run back to the floathouse. It amounted to a lot of running around in the skiff and would end up taking several days. He wasn't looking forward to it, but knew he better get started soon or the fishing season would be over before he got his boat going. Besides, he was out of beer.

Chapter Three

After a few hour's sleep, I awoke to a quiet, misty morning, and peered out at the steep, tree-covered flank of Conclusion Island. Grateful that the wind hadn't come up during the night, and that my anchor had held, I laid back down to relax for a few more minutes before getting up, and promptly fell back asleep. It was mid-morning when I woke again.

This time I stayed awake, and, after a hurried breakfast, I hauled the anchor aboard and headed for Three Mile Arm under engine power. As I approached the bay, a little breeze came up so I hoisted the sails and shut off the outboard.

It wasn't much of a breeze, and under sail I was barely making two knots. But I figured I'd try to sail in, just in case Mac was around. Somehow, it seems a bit ignoble to me to be motoring in a sailboat if there's any wind at all, and the truth of it was, I thought I'd have more chance of impressing Mac with my boat if I came in under sail.

The light wind gave me just enough speed to maintain steerage, and, as I dodged the numerous kelp patches and rocks, I was glad I hadn't tried to come in during the night. Halfway into the bay, I hadn't seen any sign of human habitation. I was beginning to wonder if Mac was still living in the area, when I coasted around a small headland near the back of the bay, and noticed a floathouse tucked in close to shore, off my port side.

The float consisted of several large logs decked over with heavy planking, and appeared to be about forty feet long by maybe twenty feet wide. A little cabin, its cedar shakes weathered to a silver gray, with a roof off the back serving as a woodshed, took up about half the area. The rest of the deck was covered with an assortment of junk, including numerous fifty-five gallon drums, and a smokehouse which looked like a small outhouse with smoke curling up from around the top.

Standing outside on the float, apparently looking at the top of his boat's rigging sticking out of the water beside him, was Mac. His back was to me and, since I was barely gliding along without a sound, he hadn't noticed me yet. I got close enough to see he was wearing his usual outfit of heavy canvas "tin" pants, shiny with grease and wear, supported by wide, red suspenders over woolen long underwear, before the sound of me rolling up the jib startled him. He quickly turned and watched as I coasted alongside.

The breeze was so light I just slacked the main sheet to let the sail swing out and, still seated in the cockpit, reached out with one hand and grabbed the float, bringing myself to a stop.

Mac looked at me for several seconds in complete silence. If he was shocked, he didn't let on. Then he examined the boat for several more seconds before he finally spoke.

"Where'd you get this pretty little slip of a vessel?"

"Built it," I replied.

Once again Mac's eyes roamed over the boat before settling on me in the stern. "What for?"

That took me aback for an instant. "Well," I said, "I'm preparing for the next oil crisis."

At that his face split into a broad grin and his eyes

twinkled. "By God, if it's an oil crisis you want, you've come to the right place. I've got my own personal fuel shortage here. Not to mention another crisis," he added.

"So I noticed. How come you're standing here in the middle of fishing season looking at your boat while it rests on the bottom?"

"Its a long story," he began. "But my throat's a little dry. You got any beer on that yacht?"

"Yeah, I do. But I'm too cold for that. Sitting in this open cockpit gets chilly. How about a cup of coffee with a splash of rum?"

"Sounds good. You supply the coffee and rum and we're all set."

"Grab a line, then," I said, and tossed him the stern line.

Mac made it fast, then tied the bow and turned towards his cabin. "I'll heat up the water."

By the time I'd furled the sail, dug out the rum and coffee, and followed him into his house, Mac had an old, enameled coffee pot near boiling on a little propane burner. I sat the half-full rum bottle and can of coffee on the counter beside him, then watched from the broken-down couch across the room as he threw a handful of coffee into the pot and rinsed out a couple of mugs.

Despite his advanced age, his movements were sure and quick, and he appeared to be in reasonably good condition. In fact, he didn't seem any older than when I'd last seen him fishing down by Noyes Island. When was it, two, maybe three years ago? I wondered why he wasn't fishing now.

Mac turned the heat off under the coffee and sprinkled a little cold water on top to help settle the grounds. Then after a short wait, he filled the mugs two-thirds with coffee and topped them off with rum. "There you go," he said, handing me a cup. "Just strain the grounds through your teeth if they bother you any."

"Thanks." I took a little sip and settled into the couch, enjoying the warmth of the drink. "Now, what's this about a long story?"

Mac turned the rocking chair away from the wood-stove to face me and sat down. "I guess you could say it all started last fall when I hit a rock over in Totem Bay."

"What?" I interrupted. "You hit a rock? I thought you knew every rock in southeast Alaska."

"Well, I know that one better than I care to now. But as I was saying, I bounced off this rock over in Totem Bay. Didn't seem to do much damage and I ran over to Cook's Cove thinking I'd put the *Hazel Belle* on the tide grid there to check her out. She didn't seem to be leaking much though, and, since low tide was in the middle of the night, I decided to wait until spring when the tides've switched over and I'd be painting the bottom anyway."

"Plus", I said, "you probably got too drunk at the bar there to go on the grid anyway."

Mac scowled at me but other than that chose to ignore the comment. "Now this is where it gets interesting," he continued. "While I was there, this young guy offered to sell me a drum of gas at a real good price. Said he needed the money to fly out of there. I asked him if it was full of gas and he said it was, so I bought it."

"You didn't check it first?"

"No, I didn't check it. Not very good anyway. Besides, if someone tells you something to your face you shouldn't have to check it. Anyway, Mad Mike was tied up there beside me that morning with that big scow of his, anxious to get going. I unscrewed the bung in the barrel, saw that it was full, stuck my finger in it, and smelled that it was gas, and had Mike reach right over with his boom and set it on my back deck, easy as you please."

Mac took another swallow of his drink and went on. "Once I got home, I didn't think any more about it. I unloaded the barrel with a come-along and set it on the float. The *Hazel Belle* was leaking some, but not too bad."

"Oh," I said. "So you bounced off a rock with your boat and bought a drum of gas from a guy last fall. What's that got to do with you standing here looking at your sunken boat this summer?"

"It's like this. One fine sunny day this spring I got a little restless. So I loaded up my skiff and ran up Rocky Pass, sight-seeing and enjoying the weather. Next thing I knew I was clear up past Devil's Elbow. What the heck, I thought, might as well run up to Kake since I'm this far. I had enough gas along to make it."

"Just because someone has enough gas to get somewhere doesn't usually mean they take a forty mile ride in an open skiff," I said. "Don't I remember hearing that you had a lady friend there in Kake?"

Mac grinned. "I do happen to know a certain lady there who sometimes lets me stay over at her house," he admitted. "Anyway, when I got there the whole village seemed to be in a party mood, and there was quite a shindig going on. I stayed longer than I planned. Must've been two weeks."

"Some party."

"Yeah, it was. I've been around those Natives most of my life, and I still don't know what makes 'em tick. But I do know when the mood turns sullen, it's time to get out of there. I left in a bit of a hurry on a cold, rainy day with just enough gas to get back."

"Obviously you made it."

"Sure I did. It took me three days, though. When I got to the bottom of Rocky Pass it was too rough to get over to the 'Arm here. I had to hole up until it calmed down. Luckily I had a tarp and matches and stuff in the skiff."

"And when you got back the *Hazel Belle* had sunk. Is that right?"

"That's right. She must've been leakin' a little more than I thought."

"Didn't you have a bilge pump with an automatic float switch?"

"I did. Either it quit working or the battery ran down. I never did trust those electric gadgets."

I got up, feeling the combined effects of the caffeine and alcohol, but not knowing what they were exactly, and refilled our cups. I knew Mac was an extremely competent guy when he put his mind to it, and had refloated and repaired boats under difficult conditions before. I couldn't figure out why he hadn't made any progress on this one. Maybe old age had finally caught up with him.

"So when did that happen?" I asked. "Early June?"

"About that."

"Well, why haven't you gotten started on it?"

"That's what I'm getting at. When I saw the *Hazel Belle* sunk, I thought, no big deal. First calm day I'll skiff over to the Cove. Carl there's saving me a Chrysler Crown engine, just like mine, that he took out of another boat. They're gettin' pretty rare now, you know. Anyway, I figured I'd just get a few parts and supplies and come back and get started."

"Well?'

"Well, when I went to pump the gas out of my remaining barrel, the one that I bought from that guy at Kook's Cove, I discovered it was full of water."

"I thought you said it was full of gas."

"Nope. He'd filled it almost plumb full with water,

then poured a little gas on top. Gas floats you know. Wasn't more than an inch of gas on top. Not enough to get me anywhere."

I took another drink and mulled that over. "That guy's got a lot of nerve," I said. "Doesn't he know your life out here could depend on that gas being good?"

"I don't know what he knows," said Mac. "If I ever see him again I'll have a little discussion with him."

"I bet you will." I got up, walked outside and peed off the float, gazing again at the sad sight of the *Hazel Belle*'s mast protruding from the water.

When I came back in, Mac was still in his rocker, sipping his drink and looking surprisingly pleased with himself. Happy, I assumed, that at last he'd gotten to tell his story to someone. I was still a little puzzled, though.

"So basically," I said, "This last month or so you've just been sitting here waiting for someone to come along with some spare gas?"

"More or less," Mac grinned. "I built a little cradle on the beach for the boat once she's up, and collected some empty drums to float her with but that's about it."

Thinking about what a sodden, scummy mess the boat would be in, and what a job it would be just to get her cleaned out, I wondered why Mac hadn't gotten started. "Why haven't you tried floating her with the barrels yet? You could've had her all dried out and cleaned up and practically ready to go by now."

"Think about it," he said.

I'd always been impressed with Mac's abilities over the years, and found myself a little put out by his apparent lassitude. Especially since I knew I'd now end up helping him with what would be a hard, messy job.

"I am thinking about it," I said, somewhat petulantly. "Seems like you've been sitting around a lot thinking about it too."

Mac laughed. "True enough. But you see, that engine down in that cold water right now ain't doin' much. But the minute you get it up, it'll start rusting fast. A week out of the water without getting flushed out good and running, so it'll get thoroughly warmed up and lubricated, and it'll turn into a solid lump of rust that'll never run again."

"As it is now, as soon as I get a good battery and some gas and oil, and a few ignition parts, I can get it running in a day and it'll be fine. If I had raised the boat as soon as I got back, now I'd have to take the engine out and completely rebuild it."

"Oh," I said. "I guess I didn't think of that."

Mac drained his cup and stood up. "So now you know why I've been waiting for someone to come by."

"Right." And now, as I watched Mac walk out the door, I knew I needn't wonder about his mental abilities. As usual, ever since I'd known him, when it came to thinking, he always seemed to be about a half a jump ahead of me.

Mac reappeared, filled his cup, and sat back down, resuming the conversation. "But I didn't expect that someone to be you," he said, "sneaking up on me in a damn sailboat."

It was my turn to laugh now, which I did rather heartily. "You're lucky I wasn't a pirate. I could've sailed right up and knocked you off your float with a boat hook before you ever saw me."

Mac scoffed. "Haven't seem many of them lately. But pirate or not, I'd a been glad for the company."

In the pause that followed, I knew Mac was waiting for me to tell him about what I was doing. And I also knew he wouldn't ask outright. He'd wait until I volunteered the information, if I ever did. I didn't feel like getting into it now, though, so let the opportunity pass, and directed the conversation back to the task at hand.

"Well, the way I see it," I said, "it's kinda late for going to the Cove today. And the tide's wrong, anyway. We can get the ebb in the morning and take my boat over. Depending on how long it takes to get what you need, we'll get back tomorrow evening or the next day and get started.

Mac eyed me over the top of his cup. "Sure you want to now? I wouldn't want to spoil your fun. You might find someone else to sneak up on. A little gas for my outboard and I'll be all set."

I pretended to consider it, but really my mind was already made up. He was facing a pretty big job, especially for someone his age, and we both knew it. No doubt he could accomplish it alone, given enough time, but there might not be much fishing season left when he got going.

I'd never known him to save any money from one season to the next before, so expected he'd need to get in some fishing this summer or he'd face a mighty lean winter. And helping Mac out with his boat, I thought, would give my trip some focus. Make it seem a little more purposeful. "Sure, I'm sure," I said. "I've got nothing better to do."

The next morning found us underway in my sailboat, running with the tide. Mac had suggested he could borrow some gas and make the run in his skiff much faster while I waited, but didn't argue when I pointed out the trip would be more comfortable and safer, if a little slower, in my boat. Plus we could carry more stuff back.

So he settled onto the wooden bench in the sailboat's cockpit with a bemused look on his face, and muttering half to himself, questioned whether it actually was more comfortable than the seat on his skiff, but, after briefly noting our progress, acknowledged that it definitely was slower. I ignored his remarks, and, with the little Honda outboard droning along behind me like some giant, oversized bee, occupied myself steering the boat.

We cruised without any more talk for over an hour. Both of us were used to being alone on boats a lot and the lack of talk felt completely natural. We'd exhausted our supply of stories and idle gossip, along with the rum, last night anyway.

Presently, like so often happens, as the morning advanced a light wind came up. It was out of the northwest, a favorable direction for sailing, and as soon as I was sure we had enough breeze to fill the sails I rolled out the jib and hoisted the main. Soon the boat heeled slightly and picked up a little speed. I shut off the engine and tipped it up.

Yesterday, I'd avoided explaining to Mac why I wasn't fishing this season and what I was doing. Now, with a sunny day, a favorable wind and tide, and the boat performing beautifully, I felt inspired and confident.

With Mac listening, I expounded at some length on how I wanted to feel closer to nature again, and on the joys of sailing. When I commented on the current state of the fishery, Mac agreed that salmon trolling had definitely become more of a rat race, compared to how it used to be.

He was polite enough not to point out that part of the reason why it had become that way was because of fishermen like myself who had constantly upgraded our boats and equipment over the years, depending on catching more and more fish. Then, through a treaty process with Canada, we were given a ceiling on the number of king salmon we could catch each year. So it followed that, as our efficiency grew, the season must shrink. Which had caused fishermen like myself, but not, that I had noticed, Mac, to fish all the harder, to become more competitive.

I was sure Mac was aware of all this, and appreciated that he refrained from explaining how I was at least partially responsible for the very situation I now deplored.

By the time we approached Cook's Cove, I'd covered everything, from building my boat, including the ding-yak, to the fishing situation, to my current family difficulties. And having said all this to someone for the first time, I now found I'd gained more of an understanding about what I was doing myself. Mac hadn't said much, but I had the feeling that he approved of what I was up to.

Our timing was impeccable. The current was slack as we passed the point where the strongest tide rips form. Near shore the wind died out so I started the motor and maneuvered through the half dozen small and mostly worn out trollers working the area, and navigated in the narrow entrance to the community.

I hadn't been there for years but it looked just as I remembered. A dozen or so houses and shacks clustered around a small bay, and a state-owned float occupied by a few old fish boats and a couple of cruisers, none of which looked like they would get far under their own power, or for that matter, had tried to in recent memory. Moored to the outside end of the float was a fish buying scow, and adjacent to that sat a nondescript looking building containing a store and bar.

Mac directed me to a private float across the bay. We tied up beside an exceptionally neat-looking, tugboat-style steel vessel with a stout mast and boom, of about 40 feet in length.

"This is a nice looking boat," I said, as we made our way across its after deck.

"Yeah," agreed Mac. "Carl built it. He's pretty handy."

"I'll say. What's he do with it?"

"Oh, you know," said Mac, leading us up a ramp and along a wooden boardwalk towards a large shop. "Trips to town and such, all the things a person does with a boat in this country, plus a little towing and hauling for people."

A tall, skinny man, wearing well worn gray coveralls, watched from the shop doorway as we approached. When we neared, he broke into a grin. "Mac. You had me fooled at first. I saw that sailboat come in and thought some damn tourist was tying up to my float. What are you doing? Taking up yachting in your old age?"

"Not hardly," said Mac. "But Dave, here, is. He built her and now he's on some sort of an Alaskan holiday."

I felt myself blushing.

"Dave?" Said the man, extending his hand. "My name's Carl." We shook hands.

Mac was standing back with a trace of a grin on his face, and, feeling unexpectedly put on the spot, I quickly changed the emphasis of the conversation from myself. "That sure is a nice looking boat you got down there, Carl," I said, nodding in the direction of his float. "What kinda power you got in her?"

"Oh, an old 318 Cat," he said. "I got it used and rebuilt it."

"Those are good engines. I had one myself for several years," I said, now feeling back on more or less equal footing.

"Yeah?" Carl, looking a little puzzled, turned towards Mac. "Well, what can I do for you guys today? Or is this purely a social call?"

"You still got that Chrysler Crown?" Asked Mac. "If you do I'd like to get some parts."

"Sure. Follow me." Carl turned and walked into

his shop. In the far corner he pulled back a dusty tarp and revealed a six cylinder gas engine, complete with reverse gear and a box of spare parts. It was similar to the first boat engine I'd owned many years ago.

"You having engine trouble?" Asked Carl.

"Not engine trouble exactly," said Mac. "More like boat trouble. Right now the engine's under about ten feet of water."

"I see. Where's it at?"

"Lying alongside the floathouse."

"You need any help? I could run over and give you a hand."

"No thanks. Dave's gonna help me. We'll have her goin' in no time."

"OK. Take what you need, or I can haul the whole engine over on my back deck if you want."

"No. I'll just get a few parts and pick up the rest of it later sometime."

"OK. Well I'm in the middle of a rush valve job for someone and think I'll get back to it then. You know where the tools are. Help yourself."

Mac examined the spare parts and sent me back to the sailboat lugging a box of ignition parts and a carburetor, then busied himself removing the starter and alternator from the engine. When we had everything Mac wanted stowed away, including a spare 12-volt battery Carl had lent him, we motored across the narrow bay and tied up in front of the gas pump and store.

Mac lined up the empty five gallon cans we'd brought along. "Did you know Jim Johnson runs this place now?"

"No. Last I saw him he was tending bar up in Pelican. That was several years ago. Then I heard he moved to Wrangell or somewhere."

"Yeah. He was there awhile, then he took over this place. I think he's tended bar in every two-bit joint around southeast Alaska."

"I remember he was in that bar down in Craig that night years ago when you got in that little mix-up."

Mac gave me a quick, steely-eyed look but didn't say anything.

Jim came out of the store and unlocked a little shack containing cans of oil and such, and turned on the gas pump.

He was a little older than me, I'd guess, and short, bald, overweight and friendly. He had that good bartender trait of remembering names and faces and recognized me right off. I couldn't say I knew him well, but we'd been on a first name basis for probably over twenty years. While Mac filled three containers with gas and another with diesel, Jim and I chatted about old times.

Jim invited us in for a bowl of stew, which we gladly accepted. After eating we stayed for a beer. Other than us, the bar was empty and at the sound of an approaching floatplane, Jim quickly handed us each another beer and excused himself to meet the mail plane. I drank slowly, but, nonetheless, quickly reached the place where another beer and I wouldn't feel like going anywhere that afternoon except off to my bunk for a nap. I suggested we better get going if we wanted to make it back today. Mac agreed.

The tiny post office was attached to the store building, and on the way out I decided to see if I'd gotten any mail. A woman sorting the newly arrived mail said it wasn't ready yet. But when I turned to leave, she asked me my name, and when I told her, much to my surprise, she handed me a letter. Either the mail service was getting faster or this letter had broken the record for mail arriving from down south.

It was from my daughter. I leaned against the outside of the building and read it. It was short and to the point.

Dad,

Just talked to Mom this eve. Guess what? I'm coming to Alaska soon. With a friend. And kayaks. We're leaving Missoula tonight. We'll get off the ferry in Wrangell middle of the week. Hope to paddle to Kuiu Island. Would love to rendezvous with you somewhere. When you get this, call Mom and leave a message where and when we might meet up. I'll check with her. I'll mail this right away, special delivery. Hope you get it.

Love,

Heather

I reread the letter and stuck it in my back pocket. Mac was sitting on a bench in front of the store drinking a beer. "I'll be back in a minute," I told him. "I've got a quick call to make."

Stepping into the store, I spotted a phone just inside the door and dialed my wife's number. As I expected, she wasn't home. I left a message for Heather on the machine, telling her to look for me at Mac's floathouse at Three Mile Arm for the next week or so. She'd fished with me for several seasons and was familiar with charts and navigation so I knew she wouldn't have any trouble finding the place. I just hoped she was more seaworthy in her kayak than I was in my ding-yak.

As I came out, Mac stood up with a sigh, drained the last of his beer, twisted the aluminum can almost in two, and tossed it into the bay where it slowly sank. He didn't inquire about the call I'd just made.

We walked to the sailboat, and, as I lashed a couple of the gas cans to the mast, preparing to get underway, an eighteen foot outboard cruiser came into the bay.

The driver stood behind the windshield under a small roof, but the back and sides of the steering station were open. I got a good look at him as he idled by and watched as he tied up and walked into the bar. No doubt about it. It was definitely black cap, the guy I'd tried to eavesdrop on back in Wrangell. The guy I was virtually certain I'd seen shoot that bear.

I hadn't gotten around to telling Mac the story yet, and seeing the guy again reminded me of it. I intended to ask Mac what he thought about it, but as soon as we nosed out into the strait, we began bucking into a steep chop, with spray covering the cockpit.

Mac sized up the situation as a long wet ride back to Three Mile Arm. "Guess I'll just leave the joys of sailing and communing with nature to you," he said, as he disappeared into the tiny cabin, and slid the hatch shut.

The wind was almost dead ahead so I didn't bother with the sails. I altered course slightly, so only the occasional dash of spray came aboard, and hunkered down in the cockpit. With my left hand firmly gripping the tiller, I bounced on across the straits. Once out of the tide rips, things calmed down, and as I motored along, I became engrossed in thinking about the job of resurrecting the *Hazel Belle*. By the time we reached the floathouse, I'd forgotten about the bear again.

Chapter Four

A loud metallic clang jarred me from a deep sleep. I'd been in the middle of a dream and awoke disoriented. Sitting up quickly, I banged my head on the deck beam above my bunk, then lay back down, remembering I was in my sailboat moored at Mac's floathouse.

More scraping and thumping sounds from nearby were followed by a splash. A weak light filtered in through the porthole, but that doesn't mean much in Alaska in the summertime. It felt like the middle of the night. I looked at my clock. Four-twenty. Must be low tide.

Dressing quickly, I slid the hatch open and stuck my head out. "What kinda place you runnin' here any-way?" I complained. "A guy can't even get a decent night's sleep."

Grinning, Mac looked over from his work of tying a line around an empty oil drum. "Sorry about that. Forgot you were on vacation. But, since you're up now, you might as well do something useful and lend a hand."

Previously, Mac had gotten the *Hazel Belle* and the floathouse positioned so that when the boat rose she wouldn't jam against the float. Now, working from the skiff, we firmly lashed the floating barrels to the rigging. When Mac was satisfied with the job, we went in for breakfast.

As the tide came in, the barrels floated the boat off the bottom. At high tide, using Mac's outboard skiff, we sluggishly towed the still submerged *Hazel Belle* towards the beach. When the hull grounded out again, we stopped and untied the barrels, then returned to the house for another round of cribbage and more swapping of lies, waiting for the next set of tides.

We repeated the process, each time attaching the barrels lower, and each time the tide receded more of the boat emerged from the water, until eventually, at low water, she was left high and dry, laying partly over on her side.

The *Hazel Belle* at this point was not a pretty sight. She looked no different from the dozens of abandoned derelicts one sees in certain coves surrounding the villages of southeast Alaska. The rigging was askew and one trolling pole was broken. The entire surface of the boat was covered with a thin slime and bits of seaweed.

I clambered across the slanted, slippery deck and peered into the hold. Bin boards and odd pieces of insulation floated in a scummy stew of oily water. With much difficulty, I managed to slide open the pilot house door and step inside. The floor of the pilot house was above the water, but the foc'sle was flooded. Half empty food containers, a couple of floor boards, and a wooden spoon bobbed in the bilge water. An old waterlogged mattress lay draped over the galley stove. What a mess.

I retreated to the deck and called out to Mac, who was on the beach inspecting the hull for damage, to toss up a bucket so I could start bailing.

"Oh don't go wearin' yourself out," he mumbled. He got a brace and bit out of the skiff and calmly bored an inch-and-a-half hole in the bottom of the *Hazel Belle*, then stood back and watched as the water poured out. When she was empty, he tapped a cedar plug into the hole and once again we returned to the floathouse to await the rising water.

She floated with the next tide, and at high water we towed her over and tied her to Mac's recently constructed grid.

The grid was a simple cradle affair, consisting of a few logs, beams, and uprights, bolted together and weighted down with big piles of rocks to keep it from floating. We tied the *Hazel Belle* loosely to the uprights so she could rise with the tide and settle onto the beams when necessary. Now she would float only briefly at the top of the tides, and the rest of the time sit high and dry, ready for the work to begin.

Mac and I immediately dug in, removing a sodden heap of rubble from the bowels of the *Hazel Belle*. Once we had her cleaned out, a big pile had accumulated on the back deck, although I knew it would only be a molehill compared to the contents of my troller back home.

Mac looked at the pile in disgust, then began pawing through it, tossing much of the stuff overboard. "Don't know how a guy can collect so much crap over the years," he muttered, "but at least I'll get her cleaned out now."

"Kind of a hard way to go about it, wouldn't you say?"

"That's the trouble with you modern guys, always looking to do things the easy way. Why don't you pass me that hose now and we'll get her rinsed out while the tide's down."

Sometime previously, Mac had scrounged up a roll of plastic pipe and run it down to the grid from a nearby stream. So we had running water, of sorts. It was gravity flow without much pressure, but sure beat packing water in buckets.

Mac gently tapped the plug out of the drain hole he'd bored in the bottom of the boat. I handed him the hose, and he thoroughly rinsed the engine with fresh water. Then, while I was busy scrubbing out the foc'sle, he removed the spark plugs and poured a generous amount of diesel into each cylinder.

He replaced the starter with the one we'd brought over from Cook's Cove, connected it directly to the new battery, and cranked the engine over. As the engine rolled over, he poured more diesel into the cylinders. The plug from the engine crankcase had already been removed, so the resulting mess of old oil, water, and diesel ran into the bilge and out Mac's newly created drain hole, spreading in a rainbow sheen across the water below.

"Hey," I said. "Remember that story of the *Seamaster* up by Sitka a couple of years ago."

Mac frowned as he removed the distributor. "No, What about it?"

"Milt ran on a reef and punched a hole in her. He radioed the Coast Guard and said he was sinking. By the time they got there, the boat was long gone and Milt had been picked up by another fisherman. But they noticed a little oil slick on the water and fined him $10,000 for pollution."

"That figures, but my radio don't work any more so I won't be callin' to turn myself in. Now, how about fetching that gas can that's in the skiff, then disconnect my fuel line by the filter over there, and run a hose into the can for me."

I was impressed by just how well Mac knew that old Chrysler, and by how quickly he got it running. And by the look of rapt attention on his face as he adjusted the carburetor and got her idling just right.

Later that evening, as we sat sipping our drinks back in his floathouse, he still wore a smug look of satisfaction. "Yup," he said. "That old engine didn't sound half bad after its little bath. Didn't even have one stuck valve."

I rose and looked out the window. It was now high tide. "Good," I said. "Then you won't mind doing it over. You forgot to put the plug back in and she sank again."

But Mac didn't fall for it, not even for a minute. He knew good and well he'd put that plug back in.

* * * * * * *

Dwight stopped paddling and laid the paddle across the cockpit of his kayak. Hooking his hands behind his neck, he rotated his upper body, trying to work some of the kinks out of his back and shoulders. Actually, his butt and legs were more uncomfortable, but there wasn't much he could do about that within the confined space of the kayak. That would have to wait until he got ashore, which would be soon, he hoped.

First he'd have to catch up with Heather though. He watched as she moved resolutely on, her paddle blades dipping rhythmically into the gray water, propelling her further ahead of him with each stroke. He could yell, ask her to wait, but somehow that seemed too undignified.

He unzipped his new Gore-tex rain parka, which seemed to be leaking, pulled a handkerchief from his pocket, and wiped off his glasses. Not that it would do much good. He'd never seen so much moisture--a combination of rain and fog together that left everything half obscured and dripping.

A light breeze swirled a patch of fog between them, and with a start, he realized he better catch up or he'd soon lose sight of her completely, an unnerving thought. Not that he'd be lost without her he reminded himself. The shoreline of Kupreanof Island remained vaguely discernible off to his right. Still, they should keep together. Jeez, this weather. How could it be raining so steadily and foggy too? Wasn't the rain supposed to be below the clouds? He resumed paddling with renewed vigor and eventually began to close the gap between them. Watching her continue steadily on, without so much as a pause or break in her rhythm, Dwight found himself resenting her strength, or maybe it was her assuredness to head blithely on without so much as a backward glance that he resented. Most likely that was it. Ever since they'd gotten to Alaska he'd felt somewhat off balance, overwhelmed by the sheer vastness of the place and the incongruity of modern industry and towns seemingly haphazardly interspersed throughout the wilderness. He felt out of his element. Heather, on the other hand, seemed to feel right at home, more confident and energetic than ever.

As he caught up to her Dwight put on burst of speed, then laid his paddle on the deck, and, breathing hard, coasted up beside Heather. When she noticed him she stopped paddling and smiled.

Attempting to regain his breath, he didn't say anything at first, just sat there looking at her. She was bare headed. Her thick blonde hair was wet, of course, but not plastered to her head like his own would be. It looked good wet, especially combined with those sparkling blue eyes and the color in her cheeks from the exertion of paddling. Sitting in her kayak, framed as she was by the water and wisps of fog, with a background of wild, rugged shoreline, she looked to Dwight like some sort of Nordic princess. Captivated by her beauty, he continued to gaze at her.

"What are you staring at?" She finally said.

"You. You look like the perfect picture of health and happiness, and I'm cold, tired, wet and have to pee. What do you think of stopping soon?"

"OK," She laughed. "That looks like a decent beach

just ahead."

Heather walked around, looking over the area. With a bit of scouting, they'd found a pretty nice campsite. A gently sloping beach of small rocks and pebbles was backed by a line of driftwood and a wide bench of comparatively level land, before the steep mountainside began. Their tent was pitched just behind the driftwood and beneath the canopy of a large Sitka spruce. With a little work, there would easily be room for several more tents in the vicinity.

The beach was good, stretching at least half a mile between rocky headlands, so people could take a walk without having to scramble over boulders or bushwhack. Of course it would be too exposed in a southerly wind, but she could probably find an alternate site behind one of the small islands nearby for that.

Turning back towards camp, she noticed Dwight still standing with his hands behind him, warming his backside at their fire. He'd scowled when she'd packed a small folding saw and hatchet, and began a long lecture on travelling lightly and no trace camping. She'd almost changed her mind, but, remembering what the weather could be like up here, even in the summer, had persevered, and was glad she had.

As she approached the fire, Dwight turned to meet her. "Well, what do you think? Will this place warrant a regular stop on the tour route?"

"We'll definitely keep it in mind. For calm weather at least. Plus, it's a good distance from our last campsite, and an easy day's trip on to Rocky Pass."

"Is that where we're going to meet your Dad?"

"No. Not there exactly, but near the entrance. We should get there tomorrow afternoon."

* * * * * * *

We made good progress getting the *Hazel Belle* shipshape again. While Mac busied himself with the mechanical end of things, I replaced a portion of the plank that had been damaged by the encounter with the rock, and caulked a couple of loose seams. Mac had copper paint on hand, so we painted the bottom and replaced the zincs while we were at it. Other than needing a fresh coat of paint topside, the hull was now in order.

On the next high tide we floated the *Hazel Belle* off the grid and moored her alongside the floathouse to complete the repairs.

Mac was standing atop the pilot house roof, working on the rigging, and I was down in the fish hold when I heard him mumble something about a couple of kayakers. I climbed out of the hold and watched, marvelling at the old man's eyesight, as two distant specks moving along the far shore turned our way and slowly materialized into recognizable kayakers.

Heather coasted alongside the float first, and with fluid grace, half rose, swung her legs out of the kayak, and stood on the float beside me. "Hi Dad."

Before I could respond, she grabbed her kayak by the bow, slid it up onto the float and faced Mac who was standing nearby. "Mac you look great. Haven't changed a bit. I was hoping I'd get to see you again." She gave him a long, hard hug.

Mac stood there with a surprised grin on his face as Heather relaxed her grip. I, too, was surprised by the intensity of her greeting, and a little bit hurt that she'd passed me by so quickly. She hadn't seen Mac for several years, and I hadn't been sure if she would even remember him.

Heather's as yet unintroduced friend sat in his kay-

ak alongside the float, watching the proceedings. I noticed a flicker of disapproval cross his face as Heather,
holding Mac's hand, led him towards us. I chuckled to
myself, amused by the thought that maybe he thought Mac
was her father. If this young man had romantic inclina-
tions towards my daughter, and I assumed he probably did,
he'd naturally be curious about her father. And to those
uninitiated to the Alaskan bush, Mac's appearance could
be a little shocking.

He still wore the same greasy old canvas pants that
he had on when I arrived. Cut down rubber boots on his
feet, and a gray wool shirt smeared with red bottom paint
and cut off just below the elbows, with the darker gray
woolen long underwear sticking out of the unraveling
sleeves, gave him a pretty ragged look. Complete with a
short, grizzled beard and an unruly shock of white hair, he
looked like he hadn't shaved, bathed, or changed his clothes
for weeks. And probably hadn't.

Dwight climbed out of his kayak as Heather introduced us. I didn't notice any visible signs of relief on his
face as he learned I was her father, but maybe I didn't look
as different from Mac as I might have supposed.

Mac, meanwhile, was eyeballing the kayaks. They
were built of expensive-looking lightweight plywood, and
covered with clear fiberglass and a gloss varnish finish
which highlighted the grain of the wood. Trim and functional looking, they were modern, attractive craft that
maintained something of a traditional, timeless appearance.
I liked them. Apparently, Mac did too.

"Looks like you got decent little boats, anyway,"
he said. "Most of those things I've seen in the last couple
of years look more like bright colored plastic bathtub toys
than anything else."

"Yeah," I agreed. "Where'd you get these, Heather?"

"Oh, four of us from school ordered the kits and built them in a friend's shop. It took us longer than we expected, but they turned out nice."

With that said, no one seemed to know what to say next. The silence deepened and we all stood there feeling just a little bit awkward. A raven flapped overhead, emitting a single, harsh croak that broke the spell. "Well," said Mac, turning towards his cabin, "come on in and have a cup of coffee."

"After you." I took up the rear and followed the rest of them to Mac's cabin. Dwight peered around the float intently, trying to take everything in. He was a decent enough looking fellow, I thought. Probably a year or two older than Heather, and with his glasses and short, thinning hair, he had something of a scholarly appearance. Pausing just outside the door, he examined several rusty traps hanging by their chains under the eaves. Then he reached out and touched one, as if making sure that's what they really were, before stepping inside.

Mac stirred the coals in the bottom of his barrel stove, tossed in a couple of pieces of wood and closed the door. "There, that should take the chill off. Now, what'll it be? We got water, beer, and coffee."

"A beer sounds good to me about now," said Dwight. "How about you, Heather?"

"No. Nothing for me, thanks."

"Make that two," I said.

Mac brought a six-pack in from the woodshed, pulled a can off for himself and set the rest on the table. Dwight and I helped ourselves. Heather stood off to one side, looking out the window. Her profile, just then, reminded me of her mother, and I felt that now familiar pang of doubt and worry about her, about us.

"So how's your Mom doing?" I asked. "Did you stop and see her in Seattle?"

Heather turned. She really did look a lot like her mother. "We spent the night with her. She's doing fine. She said to say hello if we found you."

Something about her tone of voice discouraged me from pursuing that subject any further, so I quickly changed tacks. "I was surprised to get your card. Last I heard you had a summer job with that outfitter."

"A guy's filling in for me right now. I'm just taking off a couple of weeks to research this. What I really want to do is set up a kayak touring business here in southeast Alaska, starting next year."

"Oh." I turned towards Dwight. "And are you part of this plan?"

He stole a quick glance at Heather, and replied hesitantly. "I'd have to say, at this point in time, my participation in the venture is somewhat uncertain."

"Must be a lot to do, setting up a business like that; getting permits, kayaks, supplies, and advertising. I suppose you'd have to have some sort of insurance in case someone got hurt. Can you arrange all that while you're still going to college?"

I could tell Heather didn't appreciate me questioning her abilities.

"I'm looking into all that. Things are really falling into place. I just talked with this man in Wrangell, an old friend of a friend of mine. He's real interested and could supply a lot of help in the logistics and business end of things, while I lead the tours. He's even got his own airplane. In fact, he's going to fly out here tomorrow to meet us, and fly us around." She looked at Mac. "I hope that's OK."

"Hell, for two months I sat here hoping someone

would come by. Now I've got a yacht and kayaks, might as well have a plane too. I should start my own tourist business."

He drained his beer and stood up. "I'm gonna finish up outside before it starts raining again. You folks make yourselves at home. Move your outfits right inside. You can bed down here."

"Thanks, but that won't be necessary," said Dwight. "We wouldn't want to put you out. We can set up our tent nearby."

"Don't worry. I'm movin' aboard the *Hazel Belle* for the season anyway. I'll sleep there."

"OK," said Heather. "That'll be nice."

They began unloading their kayaks, while Mac and I went out to finish our projects on the boat. "I guess I'm gonna' have to have a talk with that daughter of mine."

After a long pause, Mac finally answered. "Why's that?"

"Her poor taste in men."

"Now that young fella didn't seem that bad."

"It's not him I'm worried about. It's you. Carrying on with old men like that is disgusting."

Mac laughed, "You're just jealous."

"True enough, I suppose." I left Mac chuckling to himself and resumed work in the hold. Once I finished up there, I began work on the running lights-I figured that was something Mac would probably overlook. Taking them apart, I cleaned the connections, and generally fiddled around until they came on.

Soon, true to Mac's prediction, it began to rain. He declared the rigging good enough, so we knocked off for the day and went inside.

Dwight sat in a chair, reading a book. Beside him, Heather was bent over a chart spread on the floor, measuring distances with a pair of dividers. I knelt down beside her. "Tell me about your touring plans."

"I have several ideas. And we'll tailor trips however any particular group wants, within reason of course. It's not like floating down a river, where you just go from point A to point B. There's so many options of where to go around here."

"That's for sure. You could paddle around all summer for years without seeing it all."

"Right. That's why I'm going to pick three or four basic trips to offer. I think baseing out of Wrangell will work. We can meet people at the airport or ferry, put them up for a night, Anthony can help with that, then take off on a one or two week trip from there."

"So where will you go?"

"One option for a standard one week trip could be around Etolin Island. That's a steep, rugged island with lots of bays and sheltered waters, about the right distance around. Another option, if some preferred, would be across the Stikine River delta, maybe upriver a ways, then along the mainland to LeConte Glacier, although there may be some tour boats there."

"Uh huh, and what about out this way?"

"I want to offer a longer, more adventurous trip too, like up through Rocky Pass and around Kuiu Island. That trip would have a bit of everything, from small inside passages to ocean conditions."

My heart fluttered at the thought of her paddling around Cape Decision, on the southern end of Kuiu Island, in such a tiny craft. "You're not planning on doing that now, are you?"

"No, we don't have time now. We're going to check out Rocky Pass while we're in the area. I've heard there's a lot of logging up towards Kake, and I'm not sure how that would go over with the kayakers. Mostly, I'd like to stay in the more pristine areas."

"I think you'd be doing a disservice by avoiding the logged areas," said Dwight. "It would be good to heighten the awareness of people to current land use policies. The more people see what's going on in our National Forests, see all the clear-cuts, the better. Then they can influence Congress to stop it."

"Well, maybe."

Mac spoke up from the kitchen, where he was working on dinner. "Won't do you any good in some places."

Dwight turned. "Why not? This is all part of the Tongass National Forest, isn't it?"

"Here it is. But not everywhere they're logging. Some's Indian land, awarded in the Native Land Claims Settlement Act. And they're logging the hell out of it."

I could see that Dwight had trouble with that. Probably had visions of some Native praying to the spirit of an ancient cedar tree, before chopping it down to carve out a dugout canoe. Of course maybe some did, for all I knew. But I'd seen logging on Native lands for several years now, and knew it was at least as bad as anything done in the National Forest.

"I'm certain they must have suitable environmental standards," he finally said.

Mac didn't bother to reply.

"Any way," said Heather. "We'll go that way for a look around. Rocky Pass looks interesting on the chart and I've never been there. I don't think it's necessary for me to actually have camped everywhere we may go in the future, though. Mainly I just want to get used to living out of the kayaks and getting around these waters in them. Camping's not really much different whether you're hiking or floating a river, or whatever."

Here I saw an opportunity to ask what had been bothering me ever since I'd heard about this scheme. "Since you fished with me several seasons," I began, "I know you can navigate, and are familiar with these waters, and what they can be like when the current meets the wind and swells at a place like Cape Decision, and all that. But do you have much kayak experience? Are you seaworthy in one of those things? Can you roll over?"

Heather laughed. "What do you think I've been doing in Montana these last few summers? I've rolled over plenty, white water kayaking. Of course, righting a heavier, touring kayak is more difficult in a way. I've practised that too, but I doubt it can be any scarier that hurtling down a river upside down with boulders rushing past your head."

"I don't think you have to worry about her kayaking abilities," Dwight said.

"Well, that's good to know." I didn't even want to think of her hurtling down any rivers upside down, boulders or not, but their confidence reassured me, and I began to regard the plan as a feasible one.

Dwight went back to his book, while Heather I and examined the charts. I pointed out several places I felt would be interesting, or provide good campsites in different weather conditions.

Mac dumped a couple of jars of home canned meat into a pot of steaming vegetables, and soon the aroma of a hearty-smelling stew made us all hungry.

Typical of the long, Alaskan summer days, it was nearly ten o' clock by the time we finished dinner.

Chapter Five

Morning dawned with the promise of a nice day ahead. High, scattered clouds replaced the solid overcast which had stubbornly clung to the tree tops for days. The sun worked its way through, and began drying things off. Despite the improved weather, no one seemed anxious to get anything done. We all converged in Mac's kitchen for a late breakfast, and were lingering over second cups of coffee when I detected the faint drone of an approaching plane.

As the sound increased, we went out to watch. The small float plane circled twice, then landed and taxied up to the float. The pilot, a young man with swept back hair, wearing the lightweight Filson jacket often jokingly referred to as an Alaskan tuxedo, stood on the pontoon as we caught the wing tip and maneuvered the plane into position. I knew I'd seen him somewhere before. Recently.

Heather greeted him enthusiastically and introduced us. Anthony Richardson. The name wasn't familiar, but, right off, I didn't think I liked him. Wanting to talk a little, and see if I could place where I'd seen him, I suggested we all go back in and finish our coffee.

It struck me as I took my first sip. I'd seen him in that bar in Wrangell, talking with black cap, the guy I'd seen shoot that bear, and seen again just recently in Cook's Cove.

I tried to recall what little of their conversation I'd been able to overhear. Black cap had seemed a little worried, had said something about too many people around. Anthony had replied that the market was there now. Then he'd gotten in a truck behind the tavern and left with that oriental man.

Thinking this over, I paid scant attention to the small talk going on around me, adding only the occasional, feeble comment when required. Mac wasn't saying much either, just sitting quietly off to the side, while Heather and Anthony did most of the talking.

During a lull in their conversation, keeping a careful watch on Anthony out of the corner of my eye, I casually said, "Say Mac. Why would someone shoot a bear, then leave it after making a cut on its abdomen?"

If I had expected Anthony to jump out of his chair, I would've been disappointed. He might have reacted a little, I couldn't tell. Mac leaned back and regarded me thoughtfully, but before he could say anything, Dwight cut in.

"Gallbladder."

"Gallbladder?" I asked. "What about it?"

"There's a growing trade on the black-market in bear gallbladders. It's highly illegal and totally disgusting, but can be very profitable."

"Why would anyone want a bear gallbladder?"

"They're in great demand in Asia. The orientals dry them, then grind them into a powder which they sell for an astronomical amount. They think it helps their sex life."

"That's weird," said Heather.

"Yes," agreed Dwight. "And for that they've virtually exterminated all the bears in Asia, except for a few in cages, where they extract their bile with a syringe. Now, with their economy so strong, they can afford to pay high prices for bear parts in the U.S."

"That ain't right," muttered Mac.

"How do you know all this?" I asked.

"Recently a large poaching ring, operating in several western states was apprehended. The subject received considerable coverage in the environmental press."

Anthony, who had remained impassive during the conversation, now turned to me. "Why did you bring that up, Dave?"

"Well, recently I saw a guy shoot a bear. I looked at it later and saw the slit he'd made. As far as I know, he never came back. I've been meaning to ask Mac about it, but forgot. I don't know why it just now popped into my head," I lied.

"Are you sure he didn't eviscerate it, planning to come back later and retrieve it, maybe with some help?"

"It definitely was not gutted out."

"I see. I'm sure there's some other explanation for it. I've never heard of anything like that up here."

"He's probably right," said Heather.

Dwight looked at her. "Possibly."

It seemed like Anthony had attempted to lightly dismiss the incident, but, when no one else asked any more questions, he couldn't quite leave it alone.

"Just in case," he said, "did you get a good look at the guy? Could you identify him?"

"I don't know, why?"

"I was thinking. Maybe I should report it when I get back to town. Our wildlife are a valuable asset to the tourist industry. I'd hate to see anything like that get started. Where'd it happen?"

"Oh, it was south of Wrangell, but I didn't really see the guy. He was a long ways off. I heard the shot and could see a tiny figure way down the beach. I looked at the bear later."

"Did you see his boat or anything?"

"No"

"Not much to go on, then, but I'll pass it along when I get back. And speaking of getting," he said, smiling at Heather, "we better get going."

Dwight sat in the back alone, and Heather climbed in beside Anthony, up front. The Cessna sputtered to life, and after a brief warm up, roared across the bay and lifted off. Once the racket subsided, I turned to Mac. "I don't think I trust that Anthony."

"Why not?"

I told Mac the whole story of seeing the guy shoot the bear, and how the next night I'd seen him meet Anthony in the bar, and how I'd eavesdropped on them.

"Now, after what Dwight just said, it all makes perfect sense. I bet Anthony is the middle man, supplying the buyers, probably hired that other guy to do the killing."

"I guess it could be possible. One thing for sure, bear season don't open up until September, for whatever that's worth. Why'd you tell him you didn't get a good look at the shooter?"

"I don't know, exactly. Guess I just didn't want to show all my cards. Did you see how anxious he was to know if I could identify him?"

Mac scratched his head and looked at me questioningly.

"And I'll tell you something else," I said. "I just saw that other guy again. He came into Cook's Cove just as we were leaving. In that little outboard cruiser."

Mac scratched his chin this time. Then cocked his head a little to the side and looked at me. "Well, that makes an interesting story, but what are you going to do with it? It's all just circumstantial evidence, as they say, and not even much of that."

"I don't know. Nothing probably. The point is, though, I have a feeling about that Anthony. I don't trust him, and I don't want Heather to have anything to do with him."

"If he's involved in what you think, why would someone like that want to get in the kayaking business?"

"How should I know? I just hope I can persuade Heather to find a new partner."

I thought it over while they were off on their airborne sightseeing trip. True, I had no idea why he'd want to get involved in the tourist business. On the surface, it seemed incongruous with poaching, but still, to me, it all added up. I'd just have to talk with Heather, be supportive of her plan in general, but encourage her to find someone else. Timing could be critical, probably the sooner I brought it up the better. Mulling it over, I picked distractedly at some corroded wires on the *Hazel Belle* and, sooner than I expected, I heard the returning airplane.

Climbing out, Dwight appeared thoughtful, but Heather looked absolutely radiant. Eyes sparkling, color in her cheeks, she was obviously exhilarated by the thrill of the flight. She looked great, but my heart sank as I watched her take leave of Anthony. She gave him what seemed an overly affectionate hug, and, though I couldn't hear, I'm sure, a promise to meet again soon. Dwight stood stiffly off to the side. We watched as Anthony banked out of Three Mile Arm and disappeared. When Heather turned, I recognized the look in her eyes, as probably only a parent can.

I'd first noticed it when she was thirteen and developed a crush on a neighbor boy, two years her senior. It was a look of excitement, and infatuation, and longing, but also something more. Nearly hidden, lurked a sense of tragedy, as if somewhere, deep in her unconscious, she understood pain would follow. That affair had not gone well for her at all, and I had a foreboding that this wouldn't either.

She flashed me a big smile as she walked past and into the cabin, Dwight trailing along behind. I remained standing on the float, listening as the sound of the plane nearly faded away, then increased slightly for a brief time, and finally faded out entirely. That's odd, I thought, he's turned and is heading south, out Sumner Strait.

* * * * *

Swinging low over No Name Bay, checking for bears on the grass flats out of habit, Anthony smiled to himself. What a stroke of luck. Just as he was looking for something as a cover for his activities, a beautiful girl shows up on his doorstep, talking about setting up a kayak touring business.

Who had she said she was friends with? Sharon? He hadn't even seen Sharon for a couple of years, not since they were together for a while in Homer that summer. Sharon the Heron he'd thought of her, because she had such long legs, and was always off watching those damn birds.

Now Heather shows up, looking like she just stepped off the pages of a glossy outdoor magazine featuring delectable young coeds at play in the wilds. The more he thought about it, the more he liked it. He'd help her set things up, and who knows, maybe they'd even make a little money. The tourist business was expanding anyway, and to a certain extent would cramp his style, so he might as well get in on it. Work things from both ends. What better cover could he ask for?

And as for Heather herself, well, that would just

add icing to the cake. Then a shadow of doubt crossed his mind. Something about her old man didn't seem right. Suddenly he wondered if he was being set up by an undercover team posing as father and daughter. She would try to get close to him, gain his confidence and learn what she could, while the rest of them snooped around. Maybe that old coot on the floathouse was in on it too, his shack full of electronic surveillance equipment and they'd just planted a bug on him.

No. That was too far fetched. He'd had plenty of experience with cops and was good at spotting narcs. Hadn't he been the one who first suspected that agent posing as a buyer in Anchorage?

He didn't think they were cops. If Heather wanted to get close to him, fine. It might take the sport out of it, but he'd be happy to oblige her. He wouldn't tell her any more than he wanted to anyway. As for Dwight, he didn't seem too important. Probably Heather could easily be persuaded to dump him. But maybe he should keep him around for laughs. What'd he say? Highly illegal, totally disgusting, but very profitable. That was good. He'd have to remember that one.

His wave of paranoia subsided. Those people were the genuine article, just as they seemed, he'd bet on it. The only hitch was Dave. Something seemed a little off about the way he'd brought up that story of the shooting. He'd just have to keep his eye on him.

Four black bears, probably a sow and three yearlings, looked up at the sound of the plane and galloped off into the woods. Further back in the bay, a larger one casually sauntered into the trees and disappeared from sight. Good. Ray must not have been here yet. Anthony turned the plane, and at tree top height, continued along the coastline.

He followed the shore into Port Beauclerc and circled, looking for boats. Seeing none, he eased the Cessna down in a gentle landing behind an island towards the back of the bay. As soon as he coasted to a stop and cut the engine, a small gray cruiser emerged from the canopy of evergreens overhanging a narrow creek mouth.

Ray idled the cruiser alongside the resting floatplane. "What took you so long?"

Anthony grinned at him. "Had to take a pretty lady on a sight seeing trip."

"You got my supplies?"

Anthony handed him a bag of groceries and two sixpacks. "How many you got?"

"Only four." Removing the rock he had in the plastic bag, in case he had to quickly sink it, Ray passed him the bag.

Anthony glanced inside. "OK. Say, when you were south of Wrangell, a couple of weeks ago, did you run into a middle aged man in a small blue sailboat?"

"No. Why?"

"Just wondered. I met him up at Three Mile Arm, with an old timer at a floathouse this morning. Give that area a wide berth. Don't go up past Seclusion Harbor."

"What else did you see?"

"Saw a few bears in No Name just now, and several over in Tebenkof earlier. Let's do one more trip on this side, before we work around to Tebenkof Bay. I'll meet you in that spot in Affleck Canal in exactly one week."

"OK"

"And remember, if you see a big one with a nice coat, I've got an order for an exceptional black bear hide, with skull and claws."

Ray pushed his boat off. "Aye aye, general," he muttered under his breath, cracking open a beer and heading back towards the creek.

* * * * * * *

After the sound of the departing plane died out, I followed Dwight and Heather into Mac's cabin, hoping for an opening to bring up my misgivings about Anthony. I knew it wouldn't go over well with Heather, but maybe Dwight would be an ally.

Heather met me at the door. "We're on our way out for a short excursion. Mac just told us about a stream nearby that has an early salmon run. We're going to check it out. Dwight's never seen a creek full of salmon."

"Oh, how far is it?"

"Only a couple of miles. We'll be back this evening."

"I think I'll go along. If you don't mind."

Heather looked doubtful. "We're taking our kayaks."

"That's OK. I've got my own."

They watched as I unfolded my ding-yak and attached the ends.

Heather examined it and smiled. "Cute. Are you sure it will hold you?"

"Sure I'm sure. As long as you don't lead me through any rapids or waves."

"It should be fun. Let's go."

"Just a minute." Ducking into the sailboat, I slipped into my rubber boots and jacket, and grabbed my rifle. I worked the lever to make sure the firing chamber was empty, and loaded five cartridges into the magazine.

Dwight eyed me skeptically as I emerged with the gun. "Is a firearm necessary?" He asked.

"No, probably not. But if there's salmon in the

creek, there'll be bears around."

"Aren't these black bears on this island? I understand they're quite timid, and very seldom bother anyone."

"That's right," I said, as I eased myself into my dingyak, "very seldom. I just like having it along. Don't worry, I won't do anything foolish."

Heather was already in the lead. Dwight soon caught her, but since my boat has a shorter waterline, which gives it a slower hull speed, not to mention an older, heftier occupant, I had difficulty catching up. They waited for me, and slackened their pace to keep from leaving me behind again.

We skirted along kelp beds and boulders, and after twenty minutes of paddling, ghosted into the head of a small bay. The tide was nearly full, so we were able to paddle directly into the creek. A number of eagles wheeled overhead, and sat watching our progress from surrounding trees, and a flock of gulls rose noisily from a nearby sand bar.

From the amount of birds present, I guessed the salmon must be in, but so far we hadn't seen any. Most likely, they'd left the creek mouth where they often congregate, and ascended with the tide. Heather led us upstream until our way was blocked by a large log. We beached there and proceeded on foot.

The terrain here was typical of southeast Alaska. An expanse of beach grass at the head of the bay quickly gave way to thick forest of hemlock and spruce trees, towering over dense patches of blueberry and salmonberry bushes. A well worn game trail skirted the worst of these thickets, and followed the course of the stream.

We paralleled the creek for a hundred yards, then broke out onto a small gravel bar beside a deep pool. Salmon were in the pool. Occasionally one would jump clear of the water, or break the surface with its dorsal fin, or we'd get a glimpse of a few circling, but due to the depth, we were unable to get a good look at them.

"Let's look farther upstream," said Dwight, striking out ahead. The trail left the creek bank again and cut through the woods. Heather and I trailed behind. I figured this would be as good a time as any to discuss Anthony.

"You know," I said, "about you going..." I was interrupted by a loud 'woof'. Dwight froze about fifteen yards in front of us. Then came a scratching sound, and, beyond him, and a bit off to the side, two small bear cubs scrambled up a spruce tree. Revealing herself now, a large sow stood on her hind legs on the trail thirty yards in front of Dwight and growled.

As the bear roared and gnashed her teeth, we stood poised, nobody making a move or a sound. Then, in a flash, she dropped to all fours and charged. Dwight immediately turned and ran as fast as a he could back towards us, the bear gaining on him with each leap.

My rifle had been slung on my shoulder, nearly forgotten until then. Now I tried frantically to get it into position while I jacked a shell into the chamber and stepped sideways. I couldn't shoot from the trail because Dwight was directly between me and the rapidly approaching bear. I hoped I could get off a shot before she caught him.

Just as Dwight got even with me, he tripped over a root and went sprawling into the brush on the other side of the trail. He hit with a crash and began desperately flailing around, trying to regain his feet.

At the commotion, the bear, now only forty feet away, came to an abrupt stop, cocked her head and, looking just like a dog puzzling over something, regarded Dwight. I had my front bead resting squarely on her nose, but, thinking of the cubs in the tree, didn't want to shoot if

I didn't have to.

"Easy," I said to Dwight. "Get up real easy and start down the trail. You go too Heather."

The bear stood its ground and watched as Dwight rose shakily to his feet, adjusted his glasses, and, without a backward glance, began tiptoeing down the path as if he were walking on eggs.

"OK bear." I said, out loud. "Just hold still and we'll leave you alone." Cautiously I lowered the rifle partway, and keeping my eyes on her as much as possible began inching my way backwards. I let out a sigh of relief when, after I'd made about twenty agonizing feet, constantly shifting my gaze from my next step to her impassive face, she calmly turned and disappeared back up the trail.

With a trembling thumb, I eased the hammer down, and turned and caught up with Dwight and Heather. We didn't relax until we got back to the kayaks.

Heather held Dwight at arm's length and looked him over carefully. "Are you sure you're OK?"

"I'm fine." He answered woodenly.

"Well, in that case," I said, "lets head back. I've had about all the fun I can handle for one day."

When we trooped into the cabin, Mac was engrossed in a magazine that Dwight or Heather had brought along. He looked up, smiling. "Its amazing what young kids do for excitement now days; diving off bridges with rubber cords tied to their ankles, jumping out of planes with boards on their feet, climbing frozen waterfalls, soaring off cliffs with gliders." He shook his head. "And how was your trip?"

"We had some excitement of our own," said Heather.

"It was very educational," I said, dryly.

Mac put down the magazine. "Educational, huh?

What'd you learn?"

"Learned a brand new way for stopping a charging bear."

"Now what might that be?"

"It's like this. If a bear's chasing you, right before he gets ya, dive into the thickest brush available and thrash wildly around. This confuses the bear so much it just stops to watch, then loses interest and walks away."

Heather and I were grinning, but so far, apparently, Dwight had failed to see the humor in the story. Mac looked at each of us in turn. "So Dave, do you have first hand knowledge of this tactic?"

"Sure do. Just witnessed it myself, and I can attest that it worked perfectly."

"That sounds mighty interesting. I wish I would've seen it for myself."

"Well, I wish you would've too, standing right there beside me with that old 45-70 of yours. I can tell you that little 30-30 in my hands felt awfully puny with that big old sow closing in on Dwight."

"Yeah, that 45-70 makes a dandy close range bear gun."

I think Dwight was growing a bit defensive at this point. "Bear gun," he said, scornfully. "I got too close to those cubs, and she was just doing what comes naturally to protect them. As soon as she determined I was no longer a threat, she left us alone."

"Trouble with that," said Mac, "is sometimes they chew on you a while before determining you're no longer a threat."

"Be that as it may, I find the notion of a bear gun offensive. I think so-called sportsman flying up here to shoot a bear, so they can take home a trophy, should be outlawed. Probably bears have an undeserved reputation for being aggressive and following through with an attack because they've been shot first. I don't know why anybody would want to shoot a bear. Unless they absolutely had to," he added.

I guess he didn't realize that was bear meat we'd eaten for dinner last night, but, in order to make another point, I decided to let that slide. "I do," I said. "And you said it yourself this morning. Gallbladders. Speaking of which, to change the subject slightly, there's something that's been on my mind all day."

I proceeded to tell again the whole story which I'd earlier related to Mac. Heather interrupted me as I was about to finish. "I thought you said you didn't really see the guy with the gun."

"That was what I said, but actually I did see him."

"Even if it was him you saw with Anthony, that means absolutely nothing."

"I didn't say I could prove anything, but it adds up to me. I have serious doubts about Anthony, and hope you'll reconsider getting involved with him. Other than that, I'll be happy to support you any way I can."

Heather's face turned red. "That's the most ridiculous..." She stopped herself and looked around. "Excuse us please." Then she got up and walked out the door.

Feeling awkward and embarrassed, I followed her out. She turned on me immediately.

"That's the most ridiculous idea. You've barely even met him and you're trying to tell me not to get involved with him. You don't know anything about him."

"Well, I know what I think."

"You don't know anything about people. You don't even know your own wife," she said accusingly.

"What do you mean by that? She's the one who left."

"Sure she did. And you don't even know why."

"I guess she wanted more independence," I said lamely.

"See! She's begging for your attention and you don't even know it."

"Moving out is a funny way to ask for attention."

"You're hopeless! Short of turning herself into a damn fish or a boat, moving out is all she had left to get your attention. You've done nothing but take her for granted for years. You've spent more time caressing your stupid boats than her. I bet you've spent a hundred times more hours thinking about salmon in the last ten years than about Mother."

It's not an exaggeration to say I was left speechless by this turn of the conversation. But Heather wasn't quite through.

"So don't try to tell me who to get involved with when you can't even figure out your own relationships. You better fix your own life before you try to tell me how to run mine." She stalked across the float, got into her kayak, and paddled off.

I stood riveted in place, stunned by what she'd just said. At first I tried to dismiss it, but then I had to admit that Heather was at least partly right. In recent years, up until Karen had moved out, I undoubtedly had spent much more time thinking about salmon than her. Maybe she really did want more attention, instead of independence, as I had so conveniently supposed.

I wandered back into the cabin, bewildered by it all, wondering how I'd gotten so quickly from joking about that bear chasing Dwight, to my misgivings about Anthony, to being chewed out by my own daughter for neglecting my wife.

I opened a beer and slumped down in the chair.

Mac and Dwight were apparently engaged in a philosophical discussion about bears. "OK," said Dwight. "I'll grant that if it's ethical for anyone to shoot a bear, it would be someone like yourself, living out here and needing the meat. But what I don't understand, according to your views, is why it's OK to trap a fur-bearing animal, such as a mink, and sell its fur for a rich lady's fashion statement, and not OK to shoot a bear, undoubtedly a less painful death, and sell its gallbladder to, at least theoretically, enhance someone's sex life."

"Well," said Mac, "one's legal and the other's not."

"Yes, but we're talking about more than just laws here. Laws can be changed. And while our opinions may differ, I do respect your experience, and am truly interested in your personal views."

Mac leaned back and regarded him thoughtfully. My mind was still in such a turmoil I'd only been half heartedly following their conversation, but now I was interested in Mac's answer. He remained silent for so long I began to think he wasn't going to respond at all.

Finally he said. "This is one case, I believe, where the law got it right, maybe just by accident. It's hard to put into words. For thousands of years man and animals have evolved together. Earlier cultures all had certain codes of behavior for relating to animals; what was considered proper and respectful and so on. For the most part, modern men have forgotten this."

"Now, if you live out here long enough, no one else around for fifty miles, no sound in winter but the blizzards and the wolves howling, at times killing certain animals for various reasons, other times leaving them alone, sometimes feeding them, sometimes depending on them to keep you fed...if you live in the wild long enough, you develop a sense or feel of what's right when relating to animals, much like you have a sense of how you should be towards other people."

"There's more communication between man and animal than you might think. Only it's at a level most people don't develop any more. I think some animals, somehow, voluntarily participate in being prey, and others, including man, in being predators. And if some are killed by others in a certain way, and for a certain reason, it's OK. It doesn't offend the soul, so to speak, of the prey species. But for other reasons, it might not be OK." He paused. "You spend several years out here by yourself and you might get an inkling of what I'm talking about."

"I've only got one question," said Dwight. "Since you mentioned man and animals evolving together, do you think, then, that things could change? That what once was a proper way for men to relate to animals might not be proper a few generations later?"

"I suppose so. As far as I know, nothing stays the same forever. And I see what you're driving at, but remember this; Presently mankind kills or permanently eliminates many times more furbearers through agribusiness, and developers spreading concrete, than a handful of trappers do, working their lines sustainably year after year."

For once Dwight was momentarily at a loss for words. I could have told him that debating Mac, if he were in the mood for it, was not an endeavor to be taken lightly. He lost a little of his cool, academic manner now. "But I'm thinking of the pain and suffering of the individual animal, caught and held by the paw until it freezes or is clubbed to death."

Mac rose to his feet. "Fine, think of it all you want, even though you don't know anything about it. But I'll tell you this: If I was a bear or a mink I'd rather take my chances getting shot or trapped up here where there's still room to live, than down below amongst all the houses and people, no matter what they may think about my pain or suffering. Now I've flapped my gums enough for one day." With that said, he opened the door and went out to his boat, leaving Dwight sitting there, pondering his words.

I got up to leave too. "By the way," I said, "Heather went for a little paddle. I think she'll be back in a while."

I laid in my bunk for a long time, listening for Heather's return. Eventually, I heard a soft splash and creaking on the float as she pulled up her kayak and walked into the cabin.

Now I tried to get to sleep, but my mind was racing with thoughts of all that had occurred today. I had too much to think about. During the night I drifted in and out of a fitful sleep, mixed with a confusion of dreams; where bears chased people, people chased bears, my wife turned into a bear, then a trapped mink, and Heather riding a bear chased me, while Anthony smiled in approval. It was all a big nightmare, and I got up in the morning feeling more tired and confused than when I went to bed.

Chapter Six

Heather greeted me coolly in the morning. I lingered around while she and Dwight loaded their kayaks. I hadn't gotten over how angry she'd been with me, so didn't press her.

When it came time to leave, she gave Mac a big hug. "Good bye Mac. It was great seeing you again."

Mac grinned. "Are you coming back this way?"

"No, we'll go up Rocky Pass for a day or two, then back towards Wrangell. I'd like to loop down through Snow pass and take a look at the north end of Etolin Island, if there's time."

"You stop in if you're ever in the area. Make yourself at home if I'm not around."

"OK."

"It's been a pleasure to meet you, Dave," said Dwight, shaking my hand.

"Same here."

Heather, who had been avoiding looking at me, turned and handed me a camera bag. "Here. We accidentally brought two of these. Maybe if you go down towards Cape Decision, you could take a few movies for us. We might use them in advertising."

"Sure."

She gave my hand a little squeeze, then got in her kayak, and shoved off.

Dwight shook hands with Mac. "I enjoyed talking with you," he said. "Thanks."

Mac didn't say much. I had a feeling he was about talked out for a while. We watched them depart, then Mac went back to tinkering on the *Hazel Belle*, and I retreated to my sailboat. I brewed a pot of tea and sat drinking a cup, wondering what to do next.

I guessed I'd help Mac finish up on the boat. It was about done now anyway, shouldn't take more than another day or so and he'd be ready to fish. He'd be able to get in the last half of the season, and should do fine. I'd resume my trip as planned then, except I'd sail along Kuiu Island and down to Cape Decision to take some movies for Heather before heading home.

As for Anthony, I'd just try not to think about him. After all, maybe Heather was right, and I was wrong. There wasn't much I could do about it either way. At the most, I could take my suspicions to the police, maybe something would become of it, but I doubted it. Anyway, next summer was a long way off, lots of things could happen between now and then.

The accident that changed everything happened that afternoon. Mac had an old 8-D battery on the *Hazel Belle*, which was ruined now, so he decided to get it out of the way. These batteries are heavy and awkward, and about all one man can lift, especially from a cramped engine compartment in a small boat. And this particular one was worse than some because it lacked lifting handles on the ends.

Mac had it up waist high, when I stepped aboard. As the boat rocked, Mac's foot slipped and he fell. He didn't have far to fall, but the weight of the battery came down on his right hand, smashing it onto the engine's water pump.

Hearing the commotion, I hurried below. He didn't seem badly hurt, so I wrestled the battery out onto the float, nearly doing in my back in the process. When I got back inside, I found Mac standing in the foc'sle, wrapping a rag around his hand.

"Let me take a look at that," I said.

"No, it's all right."

"Come on, I'll help you bandage it." He winced as I grabbed his hand and unwound the bloody rag. It looked bad. A ragged cut angled across his knuckles and the back of his hand, where it had hit the water pump housing. Already, his hand looked swollen and misshapen.

"You might want to have that looked at. I wouldn't be surprised if there were some broken bones. Can you move your fingers?"

"Sure, don't worry about it," he said, wriggling his fingers just barely.

"OK, but let me put on a better bandage."

I got a first-aid kit out of my sailboat, and met him on the float. First I dabbed away some of the blood. Fortunately the engine was comparatively clean where he'd hit, so the wound wasn't covered with grease. I carefully folded a flap of torn skin back in place, put a compress over the cut, and bound his whole hand with gauze and an ace bandage.

"Thanks Doc," he said. "I suppose this calls for a shot of pain killer."

"I'm sure it does."

Mac had stocked up on beer when we'd been in Cook's Cove, but had refrained from buying any whiskey because, as he put it, that made it too easy to start a binge. "Drinking beer's not really drinking," he'd said.

I retrieved the pint of rum I had stashed on board, and met him in the cabin. "For medicinal purposes only," I said, handing him the bottle. He sat down and took a swig, while I started a fire in the barrel stove.

It wasn't really that cold, but the place felt so empty with Heather and Dwight gone, it just seemed too depressing for two old men to be sitting in an unheated cabin, drinking. I thought the fire might help. And it might have helped a little.

Normally, I don't lapse into melancholy when drinking, but this evening I was having trouble avoiding it. Thoughts of Karen and Heather kept rolling through my brain like surf rolling endlessly onto the beach. Mac seemed content with the silence, sitting there quietly looking out the window, but I broke it anyway.

"Mac, have you ever been married?"

"No, why?"

"Just wondered. I seem to have made a mess out of my marriage, which, I now realize, Heather blames me for. I keep thinking about it."

After a long pause, Mac replied. "I almost got married once."

"Really? What happened?"

"I never told anyone this story," he said, "but I guess it won't matter now. It happened over fifty years ago."

"I was a young man, new to Alaska, deck handing on a trap tender. We'd collect salmon from the traps and deliver them to the cannery, haul supplies from town, stuff like that. There was a gal working at the cannery, there at Murder Cove on Admiralty Island. Not many white girls worked at canneries then, mostly Indians and Filipinos, so the ones that were there had plenty of suitors."

"Well, for some reason she took a liking to me. And I didn't have any trouble falling for her. We were together every chance we got, which wasn't real often, since I was travelling around on the tender quite a bit. Things were going real well, though, and we talked of getting married at the end of the season."

"On the next run into town, I spent nearly all my savings on an engagement ring. We'd made a quicker trip than normal on this one, and got back to the cannery late at night. I couldn't wait to show her the ring. On the way to her room, I took a short cut through a warehouse, and there, coming from the little store room that was our secret meeting spot, I heard a familiar voice."

"I didn't want to look, but had to. I peeked through a crack and saw her all snuggled up with another guy, just like we'd done. I turned and walked back to the dock, and tossed that ring into the bay. Early the next morning, I left on a seiner and never went back."

"Did you ever see her again?"

"No, but I did see him again once."

"What happened?"

"I ran into him in Petersburg that fall, and picked a fight. He was bigger than me, but didn't stand much of a chance. I really tore into him, and probably hurt him worse than I should've, before a couple of guys pulled me off. I've always felt bad about that. It wasn't really his fault, he was just doing what comes natural."

"Yeah, I suppose. That's a heck of a story, though." I paused and took a drink. "Well, at least you didn't have a kid mixed up in it."

"Nope. I've never sired any offspring, that I know of. But that one of yours, that Heather, there's one to be proud of."

I couldn't think of anything to say to that. Mac must have been feeling more talkative than I thought, though, because after a short pause, he continued.

"I remember that summer, I think it was the first year you had her up here. We were fishing out of Port Alexander. Had good fishing right out front for awhile, and only a few boats around, too. Every evening we'd go in and tie to the float, have dinner, relax a bit. Soon as you'd get in Heather would come skippin' over to my boat. Uncle Mac, she called me. She always tried to talk me into taking her out fishing with me for a day, but I never went for it."

I only vaguely remembered it. "Why not?" I asked.

"Oh, the way she hopped around on the boats in the harbor made me nervous enough. I was always afraid she'd fall in or get hurt. If I took her fishing for a day, I'd be a nervous wreck, worrying about her. I don't know how you did it."

"Yeah," I agreed. "A kid can sure make you feel vulnerable that way."

The next thing I knew, I awoke with a start. I'd fallen asleep in the chair. Mac lay on the couch, snoring lightly, his injured hand across his chest. The empty bottle sat on the floor between us. I hauled myself out of the chair and outside. It was a clear night and the northern lights glimmered faintly overhead. I peed off the float, then crawled into my bunk on the sailboat.

Sunlight, streaming through my little port hole, and squarely onto my face, woke me. I got up and, surprisingly, didn't feel too bad. I smelled coffee and bacon.

Mac stood at his stove, awkwardly flipping a pair of eggs with his left hand. "Thought you were gonna sleep all day. How do you want your eggs?"

"Scrambled. Like my brain."

"In that case you can do your own." Mac moved to the table and started eating.

I poured a cup of coffee. "How's the hand this morning?"

"Seems OK. You got it so mummified with bandages I can hardly tell."

"Good." I drank some coffee and ate breakfast, and

presently my mind began to function. I realized I was ready
to leave. I couldn't face another night of sitting around
drinking and telling stories. But I was concerned about
Mac's hand, and feeling partially responsible too.

"Now here's my plan," I said. " Basically, the *Hazel Belle* is ready to fish. About all that's left to do is tie up
some gear and throw it in the water. I don't think you're
ready to gaff any fish with that hand yet, though. So lets
head over to the Cove today. I'll go in my boat and you
can run the *Hazel Belle* over. We'll ice up, get fuel and
groceries and whatever, and I'll fish a trip with you. You
just drive the boat, and I'll run the gear and clean the fish."

Mac thought it over. "I thought you were up here
on a vacation."

"As few fish as you'll be able to find, it'll be a vacation. I probably won't have much to do, just ride around
and get bored, maybe land the occasional humpy."

Mac laughed. "You think so, huh?"

The same motley little fleet as I'd seen earlier still
worked the rips in front of Cook's Cove. I slowed and
watched a while before entering the harbor. They didn't
seem to be catching much, which wasn't surprising. The
main run of cohos normally wouldn't hit here for another
couple of weeks. I expected we'd have to travel a ways to
find any decent fishing.

After mooring at the state float, I busied myself
packing a change of clothes and a few items to bring along.
Since my boat is slower, and Mac still had a few things to
sort out, I'd left Three Mile Arm before him. My trip had
been pretty slow. I'd motored the whole way, with only a
little help from the sails, and kept expecting him to catch
me. Now I wondered what was keeping him. Unfortunately, he didn't have a working radio, so I couldn't call
him. About the time I started to get worried, the *Hazel*

Belle slipped into the cove and alongside the fish buying dock. I walked over to meet him.

They lowered the ice chute, and, while Mac joked with the fish buyer, I climbed into the hold and partially filled it. Then, after taking on fuel, fresh water, and groceries, I stood in the cockpit, tying up leaders and organizing the gear, getting everything ready for the morning, as Mac worked inside, stowing our supplies and cooking dinner.

The *Hazel Belle* is an old fashioned troller, with a small round wheelhouse over the engine-the type of house that was common during the thirties, and, in this era of bigger boats and larger wheelhouses, is now jokingly referred to as a Norwegian telephone booth. Forward of the wheelhouse, she has a low trunk cabin with a relatively roomy foc'sle containing two berths, an oil stove, a sink, and a small galley table with just enough room for two.

After dinner I moved my stuff aboard, spread my mattress and sleeping bag on the empty berth, and turned in. "Wake me up ten minutes before you want the gear in the water, Captain."

The next thing I heard was Mac getting out of bed and starting a pot of coffee. Soon the engine started and I felt us getting under way. It had been a long, time since I'd been a deckhand, and I relaxed in my bunk, indulging in the luxury of letting someone else take the initiative to get us out to the fishing grounds and make the decisions. I dozed off again to the barely perceptible rise and fall of the bow, as we cleaved our way through the tiny waves of a calm Sumner Strait.

The engine slowed, which immediately reawakened me. I rose and quickly dressed. Mac stood poised at the wheel, drinking a cup of coffee and peering intently out the window. "How deep do you want to go this morning?" I asked.

He regarded me with that look of his like he was secretly amused by something. "About twenty five, I guess."

The faint beginning of dawn greeted me as I stepped out on deck. I recognized the profile of Protection Head off to our port, and behind that Mt. Calder rose like a spire in the dim morning light. Glancing around, I made out the profile of only one other troller in the distance. Mac had certainly gotten us off to an early start.

I lowered the poles, then stepped into the trolling cockpit and began lowering the first line, clipping on a leader at each marked two fathom interval. At twenty five fathoms I attached a stopper, and the tag line pulled the trolling wire away from the boat, where it trailed from the tip of the trolling pole, as if from a giant fishing rod. I repeated the procedure until all four lines were out, then, pausing briefly to admire the sun as it began to crest the jagged mountain tops to the east, headed for the galley.

About half way through a warmed over biscuit and a cup of coffee, the bell on the starboard bow-pole began jingling. I ignored it until I finished eating, hoping a few more fish would hit before I ran the lines. Then I joined Mac in the wheel house. There was just enough room for two people. "Looks like you found one stray, anyway."

Before he could answer, another pole began jerking. I put on a pair of rain pants and gloves and got down to business. Engaging the gurdy for the starboard bow-pole, I began retrieving the first line. As each leader came up, I unclipped it and neatly coiled it. When I got to the leader with the hooked salmon, I pulled it in, hand over hand, rapped it on the head with the back of the gaff to stun it, then gaffed aboard a nice ten pound coho.

I ran all four lines and caught six coho and lost one

when it twisted just as I swung the gaff. This was the part that concerned me about Mac and his injured hand. Landing salmon on troll gear requires a certain amount of dexterity. It would be virtually impossible for a right hander to switch over and do it left handed with any amount of proficiency in a short amount of time. Further more, even starting out healthy, its hard on the hand and wrist. Many seasons, after a spell of heavy fishing, I'd wince each time I gaffed a fish, as a surge of pain shot from wrist to elbow.

Mac turned the boat and trolled back along the tide streak we'd been following. Soon another pole started rattling. We caught fifteen cohos and several of the smaller, less valuable humpies in fairly short order. Then the action died out. During the time it took me to clean, rinse, and ice the fish in the hold, only one more salmon hit. It looked like the morning bite was over.

As the day progressed, we continued to work our way down Sumner Strait, picking up the occasional fish. I found myself enjoying the quiet relaxed feeling of the day's fishing, which contrasted sharply with my own trolling experiences of recent years. Part of the reason for this, I realized, was that we didn't have a radio turned on aboard the *Hazel Belle*.

On my own troller I had at least two radios on all the time, including outside speakers for when I was on deck. I constantly monitored other fishermen's conversations, and was frequently in contact with my own group of buddies, relaying information of the day's catch in coded messages, so as not to call in the whole fleet if one of us found a large school of fish. Of course other groups did the same thing, and attempting to decipher the meanings of their conversations was a constant challenge.

More than once I'd listened in as the first fisherman complained in great detail to the second about how poorly he was doing, when just by happenstance, I had the second one in sight. I may have felt smug, and thought we were doing pretty well in comparison, then felt chagrined to see the second boat pull his gear and go steaming off over the horizon, obviously called to better fishing by his lamenting partner. Then I'd go from feeling smug to agonizing over whether I should stay where I was, or, if I had a clue as to where the first fisherman was, maybe after a discreet amount of time, head over that way myself.

Now, sitting in Mac's strangely quiet wheel house, waiting for the next fish to bite, I realized how caught up in all that I had been. But, even though it was more peaceful this way, I doubted I'd leave my radios off in the future. Thoughts would continually lurk in the back of my mind that my partner was trying to call me over to some hot fishing, or that maybe someone nearby might need help. Besides that, even if it was a lot of lies and b.s., I liked the human contact of being in touch with the fleet.

Mac had never been a big talker on the radio, but maybe he had listened in more than I thought. "Do you miss havin' a radio?" I asked.

"No. I kept the damn thing turned off most of the time anyway. All that yakkin' goin' on all the time..."

I figured he'd say that. "What are you gonna do if we break down and need a tow?"

He just shrugged. I didn't tell him I'd brought along my little hand held VHF radio.

Fishing was slow all afternoon. We took turns steering and napping. If we'd been on my boat, I would've pulled the gear and headed out long ago, gone at least out to Coronation Island, or, more likely, run up the coast all night. Like a lot of the fleet now, since I'd graduated to a larger boat I found it easier and more profitable to stay out on the ocean, and didn't fish these inside waters much anymore. Mac seemed unperturbed by the slow fishing, and was uninclined to leave the area. Which, under the circumstances was all right with me. With her patched-up hull, old gas engine, and complete lack of electronics, I didn't really want to head out to sea in the *Hazel Belle* either.

As so often happens, we got a few fish at the tide change, and later that evening, as Mac steered us alongside Bluff Island, we had some action. By the time we pulled into Shipley Bay to anchor for the night, we'd accumulated a marginally fair day's catch. After dinner we sat out on the hatch cover drinking a beer and enjoying the long Alaskan twilight, until the light breeze died and the gnats, little things so small they're called 'no see ums', began biting and drove us in.

The next morning we picked up a few more cohos off Shipley Bay, then worked our way down Sumner Strait to Warren channel. Not having a working fathometer, I figured Mac would keep to the deep water, well clear of underwater obstacles, for to troll over a shallow reef or rock would result in an expensive loss of gear. But he must have accurately memorized his landmarks here.

We trolled close beside Black Rock, and two poles immediately began to bounce. At first I thought we had struck bottom but it turned out to be several salmon hitting at once. For the next two days, while I ran the gear, Mac maneuvered us in a circle between the rock and a nearby reef, without touching bottom once. It felt good to be working again, developing a rhythm. The fish were hitting at just the rate I could enjoy, keeping me busy, but not overwhelmed.

Mac didn't say much during those two days, but I could tell he was enjoying himself immensely, working this little pocket, catching fish, with no other boats on the drag.

His hand was getting better too. I'd changed the dressing the night before. The cut was healing and the swelling was down. He was a tough old goat, healing up much quicker than I thought.

The third morning two more boats joined us on the drag at Black Rock. The fishing held up for a while, but dropped off by mid morning. Just as I was bringing in a lone coho, Mac stuck his head out the door. The gaff was poised, but before I could swing, the hook pulled loose and flew back at me, clattering onto the deck.

"You might as well leave the gear up now, since you're just letting them go anyway."

I glared at him. It was the only fish I'd lost all morning. It would have to be right when he was watching.

"Besides," he said. "It's gettin' too crowded here, and old dishonest John the fishbuyer doesn't want fish more than five days old."

I gave him a mock salute and began pulling the gear. Once the leads were aboard, Mac sped up and began the four hour run back to Cooks' Cove. The old Chrysler sounded good. It hadn't missed a single beat the whole trip. I smiled as I rinsed the deck and iced down the last of the catch.

It wasn't that big of a deal for two guys, who had fished and worked on boats all their lives, to refloat and patch up a simple little troller and go catch a few fish. But, nonetheless, we'd done it. Gotten the old *Hazel Belle* going again and made a good trip. It wasn't the biggest trip either of us had made over the years, by far, but it was respectable, and I was proud of us.

About the time I had the now emptied hold scrubbed out, Mac emerged from the fish buyers office, tucking the fish ticket and a wad of bills into his pocket. I untied the lines and we moved the *Hazel Belle* over to the state float.

"Well," I said, as I rolled up my sleeping bag, "Looks like you're about recovered now. I think I'll jump ship."

Mac flexed the fingers of his right hand. "Yup, I figured you would." He withdrew some money and handed it to me. "Here, this is yours."

I looked at him in surprise. The thought of being paid had never crossed my mind. "What's that for?"

"It's your half of the trip."

I knew it would come to several hundred dollars, and was sure he could use it more than me. "I don't want it. I wasn't going along to get paid. Besides that, deckhands never get more than twenty per cent."

"You earned it, you take it," he said.

From the look on his face, I knew I better just accept it. "All right," I said. "Thanks. And, since you're so generous, I'll tell you what I'll do. I'll buy you dinner and a couple of beers at the bar."

Now he smiled. "You're on. But I'm going to change oil first, while the engine's still warm. Make sure all the contamination's out."

"OK, I think I'll go take a shower then, and meet you in a while."

I found the shower room in the back of the fish plant. It was a cold, drab place, but had lots of hot water, which I luxuriated in. Dressing afterwards, and thinking about meeting Mac for dinner, I found myself remembering another time, many years ago, when we had gone to a bar together.

It was in the town of Craig, on a Friday night. By chance, we had both finished a trip and sold our catch at the plant in town at about the same time. It had been a long, rough, tiring trip for me, and I was anxious to get off the boat for a while. I asked Mac if he'd care to join me up town.

We were sitting in a crowded bar, working on our second or third beers, and I was just getting used to sitting somewhere that wasn't rolling and pitching around, when a big fellow and a couple of followers strode in. By the way he stood there and surveyed the crowd, I could tell he was looking for a fight. I made a mental note to steer clear of him.

Later on, as Mac made his way back to our table from the rest room, he bumped into him, or maybe the guy bumped into Mac, I wasn't sure which. Looks and a few words were exchanged, then Mac turned and continued on his way. Several times after that I noticed the guy looking at us, but, soon enough, he found a different victim and they went outside to settle their differences.

Presently, we drained the last of our beers and headed back for our boats. Taking advantage of a short cut through the alley on our way to the docks, we rounded the corner of the building and accidentally ran into the tail end of the fight. For all intents and purposes, it was already over. The loser was clearly finished, but the big guy, the one who Mac had bumped into, continued to pummel him, to the apparent delight of his admirers.

I probably would've just walked on by, but was spared the decision. Mac walked right up to him. "That'll be enough," he said.

As the loser feebly attempted to regain his feet, the other guy whirled and faced Mac, a look of disbelief on his face. "What'd you say?"

Mac, who stood about as tall as the guy's shoulder, calmly repeated himself. "I said that's enough. Leave him alone. He's finished."

A smile crossed the bully's face. "Oh it's you again. Well, if that's the way you want it, then you can take his place." He cocked back his fist, but before he could deliver the blow, Mac kicked him in the left knee. The guy had that foot forward and most of his weight on that leg. At the kick, his leg buckled and he almost fell, but he caught himself, and, as he started to straighten up, an ugly sneer spread across his face. At this point, I was greatly worried.

But before the guy got straightened up, Mac's right hand flashed out of his coat in a wild, backhanded swing which spun him completely around. As the object in Mac's hand connected with the guy's skull, there was a dull thud. The guy's head jerked back, he sank to his knees, toppled over, and didn't move. Mac quickly looked at the guy's two buddies, who anxiously retreated.

For a second, no one spoke. I literally had not moved a muscle since we'd blundered onto the fight, and stood as if rooted to the spot. Mac glanced at me. "Let's go," he said, as he turned and began walking down the alley.

I hurried to catch up. "What'd you hit that guy with? I hope you didn't kill him."

Mac snorted. "He'll be all right. When he comes to. I just hit him with a sap."

"What the hell is a sap?"

Mac handed me the object. It was a tightly packed leather cylinder about a foot long and an inch or so in diameter. It felt heavy. "What's in here, lead?"

"Yeah, it's full of bird shot. That way it has the weight to knock someone out, but, with the leather covering, is soft enough that it won't break their skull."

I tapped it experimentally in the palm of my hand a few times. It definitely had an authoritative feel to it, and, I was happy to note, wasn't covered with fresh blood or bits of skull bone. I handed it back. "Where'd you get this thing, anyway?"

Mac put it in his coat. "Oh, I got it off a State

Trooper up in Tenakee Springs years ago."

"I'm almost afraid to ask what you did to him to get it."

Mac laughed. "It's not like you think. I helped him out. A few guys were drunk and causing trouble. When he tried to reason with them, they jumped him. I didn't care for those guys anyway, so I waded in and gave the Trooper a hand. When it was all over and I was nursing my sore knuckles, he gave this to me as a way of saying thanks. Said it was just the thing for dealing with unruly drunks, and saved wear and tear on your hands."

"It looks effective, all right, from what I saw of it. Do you always pack it around?"

"No," He said, "only when I think there could be a chance I might need it."

We reached the docks where our boats were tied. "I don't know about you," I said, "but I'm getting out of here real early tomorrow."

Mac didn't reply.

When I got up in the morning and got underway, he was still moored at the dock, with no lights on. I didn't see him again for a while after that, and was a little concerned when he didn't show up at some of his usual fishing spots. Then, towards the end of the season, our paths crossed again, and we spent the night rafted up together at Steamboat Bay. He seemed amused by my concern and assured me nothing further ever became of the incident.

I finished up in the shower room, put a load of laundry in the washing machine, and walked back down to the float, ready for dinner. When I came aboard the *Hazel Belle* Mac was through changing oil, and was sitting at his galley table, not doing anything that I could tell. "You ready to go? I'm about starved."

"Sure." A light rain was falling now and he slipped

into his jacket.

"Hey," I said jokingly, the incident from Craig fresh in my mind, "you still carry that sap around?"

Mac looked at me and grinned. "No. I'm too old for that now." He paused, then reached into an inside pocket and pulled out a small stainless steel revolver. "I carry this instead."

My jaw probably dropped open in surprise. "What is that, a .22 ?"

"Close," he said, slipping it back into the pocket, "It's a .22 magnum."

"Did you ever use it?"

"Sure, I use it all the time."

I must have been staring at him, because he started chuckling. "On big halibut, the occasional deer if I happen to be real close and in need of venison, trapped animals. You know you can dispatch a trapped wolf with this quite handily, if you hit him just right."

"I'm sure you could, but I was thinking more along the lines of self defense against two legged wolves."

Mac got a more serious look on his face then. "No, I've never actually used it for that. But I almost did once. I'm sure it saved me from taking a beating."

Naturally, I was intrigued. "What happened? If you don't mind my asking," I added.

"Oh, nothing much. A couple of the boys from Klawock took exception to my presence once when I was trapping at Shipley Bay. Said I was on their territory and better get out. They'd just come back from town and were hung over and feeling ornery, I guess."

"So, what happened?"

"I said I wasn't going anywhere until I felt like it, and they said they'd just have to teach me some manners. No doubt they would have too. They came from a mean family. But the next thing they knew, the bigger of the two was staring right down the barrel of that little revolver, cocked and ready to fire."

"What'd they do?"

"Not much they could do. I had the drop on them and they knew it. They just backed away, muttering to themselves."

I could easily picture it. One look into those piercing eyes of Mac's, with him pointing a gun at you, would send any sane person back, muttering to themselves. "Sounds exciting. I'm glad I wasn't there to witness it. But I doubt we'll run into any trouble tonight. We'll probably be the only people in the place."

We weren't the only ones in the place, though. The first person I noticed when we stepped into Jim's floating saloon was black cap sitting at a corner table with another guy. I couldn't help but wonder what he was doing in the area.

Jim greeted us warmly as we sat at the bar. "Evening, gentlemen. What can I get for you?"

"Couple beers to start with," I said. "Then we'll think about something to eat."

"You're in luck tonight, got some first rate steaks thawed out."

"Good. Toss 'em on the grill, along with the works. I'm tired of eating Mac's fish every day."

Mac laughed. "Didn't keep you from eating your fair share."

It felt like old times, sharing a meal and a drink with Mac after a fishing trip, with Jim behind the bar. He slid large platters of steaks and french fries on the counter, and pulled up a stool. Over dinner we told a few stories and reminisced about the past. I was enjoying myself and, with a little help from the alcohol, feeling just fine.

Part way through the meal black cap and his companion got up and left. Noticing him again cast a flicker of a shadow across my otherwise light hearted mood. "Say, Jim," I said. "Who is that guy that just left, the one with the dark hair?"

"Oh, that's Ray Thorp. Why?"

"Just wondered. I seem to keep crossing paths with him. Does he live out here?"

"No, not really. He passes through from time to time. Stays on that little boat of his. I think he's got a trailer in by Wrangell where he mostly lives. He used to come into the bar I had in town pretty regular in the winter."

"What's he do for a living?"

"I don't know, exactly. Little of this, little of that, and a whole lot of nothing, I suppose. He seems to get by. You know the type."

"Yeah, the world's full of 'em." Jim didn't volunteer any more information, so I returned my attention to dinner before it got cold.

When we'd eaten all we could, he cleared away the plates and brought us two more beers. I wasn't sure about Mac, but this would probably be my last one for the night. There was something I wanted to do, and if I was going to leave tomorrow, this might be my only chance. "I'll be right back," I said. "I forgot to check something on my boat."

Hurrying along the float, I detected the faint aroma of marijuana smoke drifting from the open port of a derelict cabin cruiser, and overheard voices, which I took to be Ray and his companion's. "I just want a ride into town, man," I heard someone say, as I passed.

Two boats further along I glanced back, and not seeing anyone, surreptitiously boarded the *Hazel Belle*.

Knowing Mac's habits, I quickly located what I was looking for. Dating from the days when all fishbuyers only
paid in cash, many old-time fishermen still kept their season's income stashed somewhere handy, on the theory that
if the boat caught fire or began to sink they could grab it
on the way out.

I opened the small coffee can and looked inside.
Sure enough, it contained several rolled up bills. I took
the money that Mac had given me, rolled it up with the
bills in the can, and replaced it on the shelf. I'd just have to
hope he wouldn't notice before I left, or better yet, maybe
he'd never notice.

Regaining the float, I chuckled to myself, a sneak
thief in reverse. As I approached the old cabin cruiser on
my way back to the bar, I heard the voices again, now raised
to a higher pitch. I slowed to listen.

"I keep telling you. I'm not going that way. I'm
going over to Chatham Strait."

"You could drop me off at Port Alexander then.
I've got friends there."

"I'm not going there either. I'm not going anywhere you want to go."

"Well, where are you going?"

"I'm going up to Tebenkof for a while."

A pause, then "Why go there? There's nothing there,
man. No people around."

"That's why I'm going there."

The conversation seemed to have reached an im-
passe as I strode out of earshot.

Rejoining Mac and Jim, I took a long drink. Jim
looked at me. "Everything all right?"

"Yeah, just a little damp. I forgot to close my hatch."

I ended up having another beer, and after that one,
knew I better get out of there if I wanted to catch the tide

the next day. I paid the bill and rose to leave. "Mac, you take care of that hand."

He grinned. "Don't worry, it's about as good as new. I'll be out there gaffing fish in a day or two."

Chapter Seven

At first light Ray idled out of Cook's Cove, then opened the throttle and planed across the water at twenty five knots. Luckily the straits were calm. Today was the day he was supposed to meet Anthony in Affleck Canal, thirty five miles away, and Anthony would be bent out of shape if he wasn't there. Especially if he learned that he'd been sitting at Cooks' Cove for the last two days.

Well, if Anthony didn't like it, too bad. He was getting tired of spending all his time out in the bush, doing all the dirty work and taking the risk while Anthony flew around, giving orders and acting like a big shot, never even getting his fingernails bloody. Another month of this, two at the most and he'd have enough money to pay off his new outboard and to last the winter. Then when the big shot, acting like some over-stuffed general ordering his troops around, tried to tell him where to go, he'd tell him where to stick it. He'd come and go as he pleased.

But in order to get enough money for that, considering how much gas he was burning up, he'd have to do a lot better than last week. Recently, for one reason or another, the hunt had not gone well. There was no one particular reason for it. He'd just had trouble getting the right shot in the right place at the right time. Either the wind had shifted and alerted his prey or, like at one stream, he'd run into a party of trout fishermen, or a plane had been circling overhead at the wrong time.

There was more to it than just going out and shooting a bear. You had to shoot one undetected and, as Anthony had repeatedly preached to him, insure that the carcass remained undetected too. It wasn't as easy as he'd first thought it would be. It would get a lot easier in September when bear season was open, though. At least then if he got caught in the act of shooting one, as long as no one actually caught him selling any parts, he could pack the hide and a little meat out and it would all be legal. Now, if caught in the act, he'd have to claim it was self defense. Which, of course, wouldn't hold up if an expert examined the carcass.

Next month he could relax a little, but not now. He had to keep his eyes and ears open, and the strain of always watching over his shoulder was beginning to wear him down. Last week had been frustrating, and, when he'd found himself only a dozen miles from Cook's Cove, after a failed afternoon's stalk, he decided to run over for a burger and a beer and a little conversation. He'd ended up staying longer than he'd planned, and now didn't have much to show for the week. And to top it off he'd had to put up with Lester pestering him for a ride into town for half the night.

Swerving around a kelp patch marking a shallow reef, Ray rounded point St. Albans. The early morning calm had held and he'd made good time on the run to Affleck Canal. Several hours remained until Anthony would arrive, so he could do some hunting. With luck, he might make up for lost time. Throttling back, he motored into Kell Bay. Once well into the bay, as was his habit, he shut off the engine and drifted for a while, scanning the shoreline with his binoculars for any sign of activity, human or animal.

Generally, when coming into a new location, he preferred to wait longer, maybe half a day, just to get the pulse of the place, and make sure no one was in the vicinity before doing any hunting. But he didn't have the time for that today. He surveyed the area once more, then seeing no indication of people around, started his engine and proceeded slowly towards the back of the bay.

Nearing the mouth of one of the creeks that fed the bay, he tipped up his outboard and coasted ashore. Since the tide was coming in, he cleated his anchor line off at about twenty feet and tied a long shore line to the bottom end of the anchor. Then he tossed the anchor off his bow and waded through the shallow water and up the beach, paying the shore line out as he went. Reaching the high water mark, he secured the rope to a drift log.

Ray sat on the log and smoked a cigarette, watching the smoke curl up and drift away, testing the breeze. The wind was light and fickle but generally seemed to be coming across the bay. He removed the caps from his scope and jacked a shell into the chamber of his 30-06, then began easing upstream. Bear sign was abundant and he expected to see one at any moment prowling the creek for spawning salmon. But after nearly a mile of stalking, he still hadn't spotted one. In one place he'd come upon the still-wet footprints of a bear where it had left the creek and walked across some flat stones just moments before. Frustrated, Ray crossed the creek and headed back down the opposite bank.

Just before breaking out of the woods onto the open beach, Ray instinctively halted behind a fringe of shoreside alders and scanned the bay for any sign of activity before making himself visible. Seeing nothing, he stepped out of the brush and started across an expanse of beach grass, walking towards the other side of the bay. He hadn't gone far when a large bear suddenly appeared in front of him. The bear was within easy range and right out in the open, a hundred yards from the shelter of the trees. Apparently he'd been lying in the tall grass. It was a tricky situation.

Ray didn't want to drop him out in the open, but if he whirled and ran it could be a difficult shot. The crosshairs of the scope rested on the bear's side as it calmly regarded Ray over its massive shoulder. Ray's mind raced as he examined the bear through the scope. No doubt about it, was a big one, its pelt was in nice condition too. Maybe his luck was turning after all. If things worked out right he could skin it and save the hide and skull and paws, there would be just enough time. That ought to make Anthony happy. Hopefully the bear would amble slowly away allowing him time to make a precise shot just before it reached the cover of the woods.

Suddenly the bear sprang away and Ray instinctively swung the rifle with him and fired. The bear fell and began growling and thrashing and tearing up the grass with its front paws. Damn. He'd rushed his shot and blown it. Instead of a hit through the ribs which would've given the bear enough time to reach the woods before it died, he'd shot high and broken its spine, dropping it in its tracks. Now the wounded and enraged bear, with it's immobilized hind quarters splayed beneath it, had pulled itself up onto its front legs and roared defiantly at Ray. He walked up to within forty feet of the beast and aimed at its head. No use worrying about the skull now. Ray's shot at the small, moving target missed its mark, grazing the animal which only served to further enrage it and increase its roaring. Rattled, Ray quickly chambered another round and fired again. The bear collapsed.

The sudden and complete silence now seemed overwhelming. Ray hunkered down in the grass, watching and waiting. He scanned the sky for planes and the bay for boats. Not seeing any he relaxed a little. His first impulse was to just forget about the bear and get out of there. Put distance between himself and the illegally killed, exposed bear. You never knew. You might sit right here for days and not see a soul, or a plane could fly over any minute. Fish and Game routinely flew around these remote areas doing salmon surveys this time of year. And Anthony would fly over for sure before too long. If he spotted the dead bear lying out here, and he surely would, he'd definitely be mad. Tired as he was of Anthony bossing him around, he wasn't sure he wanted to just take off now and have to face him later.

After a few more minutes the normal sounds of the local bird life resumed and Ray relaxed a little more. He looked closely at the dead bear. Too bad, it was a big one. But he didn't want to be standing out there skinning it the rest of the afternoon, especially when Anthony flew over. A few deft cuts with his knife and he had the gallbladder. Now he'd have to conceal the carcass. There was no way he could move it in less than several pieces, which would take too long anyway. He'd just have to cover it up.

With much effort, he managed to roll it over into a slight depression, then he began collecting grass and debris from a wide area. Twenty minutes later he was satisfied that no one could spot the dead bear unless they just about stumbled over it, which was highly unlikely. By the time an extra high tide washed the grass away or birds or another bear exposed the carcass, he'd be long gone. He glanced at his watch. Might as well go back and hang it up for the day. It was almost time for the General to come flying in.

* * * * *

Anthony gazed out his plane window at the boats

below and smiled to himself. From this height, the fleet of gillnetters working the waters in front of Wrangell looked no larger than a child's toys. He could see how each boat had positioned itself, hoping to be the one to intercept the biggest school of migrating salmon. Of course the most crowded area was right behind the fishing boundary line where numerous boats jockeyed for position to be the first in line. He was glad not to be down there among them.

When he'd first come to Alaska years ago, he'd crewed on a fishing boat, and one season of that was enough to convince him it wasn't for him. In this land of opportunity there had to be an easier way to make money than that. And there was. Later, after he'd gotten his pilot's license, he'd flown as a fish spotter for groups of gillnetters out in Bristol Bay. In the shallow waters of the bay he'd locate schools of sockeye salmon and direct his group of fisherman to them via the radio. He much preferred his lofty position over the fleet. The job paid well but the season was short and he'd expanded into other endeavors.

Now, after his rather hasty departure from the Anchorage area to Wrangell, he was just getting things going again. And they were beginning to look up. This idea of the kayak business amused and intrigued him. He still had some money squirrelled away. Maybe he should try to buy a remote piece of property somewhere as a base of activities. Could be a fair amount of money in putting up a few tourists for a while and having some charming young woman paddle them around. They could try to get exclusive Forest Service permits for guided tours in a certain area, sew the place up. That way, at least to some extent, he could control and direct some of the people in the area.

Yes, it sounded good. But he'd probably have to import some better help. He knew a couple of pros from Anchorage who, for a price, would kill anything, in short order too, and they could be trusted not to talk. Then he could branch out into the big Brown Bears over on Baronof Island. There was real money in that. Using local no-accounts like Ray was OK for a while, but a ticklish situation. On the one hand they worked cheap, but how far could he trust him? It was nice to have someone like that around for some small time jobs but what if he ends up in jail, facing thirty days for some petty crime. Would he try to buy his way out by informing on Anthony? It was a matter of balancing loyalty and fear, and so far Ray didn't realize exactly who he was dealing with. That's allright, lately Ray had been acting awfully sullen, and guys like that were easily expendable.

As he approached Affleck Canal, Anthony began his descent. Unless he was specifically scouting for something, he routinely flew higher than necessary to avoid positive identification from below. He noticed a small sailboat making its way down Sumner Strait. It looked a lot like Dave's but he was unable to tell for sure and didn't want to circle to find out. No use drawing attention to himself. Besides, he wasn't sure if it would enter the canal or continue on around Cape Decision, and even if it did come into the canal, at the slow speed it was traveling, he'd easily be out of there before it could approach them. Still, it bothered him a little. Could it be Dave and might he be following Ray? Heather should be back in town again soon and he'd have to ask her about Dave's plans. Make sure everything adds up.

After a quick, low level tour of the bay to determine that no other boats were in the vicinity and that nothing was amiss, Anthony landed and coasted to a stop. Soon Ray's boat, which was visible nearby came over to meet him.

As soon as Ray pulled alongside the plane and saw

Anthony's face, he could tell that he hadn't spotted the dead bear or the disturbed area. Old eagle eye isn't as sharp as he thinks. He smirked as he tossed the bag to him and waited defiantly for his comments on the small take.

Anthony glanced at the bag. "Slow week, huh?"

"Yup"

"Have any trouble?"

"Nope"

"Good." He handed him a box of groceries. "Were you planning on doing any more hunting around here?"

"Hadn't decided yet."

"The weather looks good for the next couple days or so. Why don't you run on around to Tebenkof while you can? You should do good there. I'll meet you in a week where we said."

Ray looked around at the sky and the water as if judging the weather. "If you say so."

Anthony smiled at him and gave him a little pat on the shoulder. "Remember, keep your eyes open for a big one with a nice pelt."

"Right."

Anthony swung up to the pilot's seat, then looked back at Ray through the open door. "Oh, and another thing, if a sailboat comes in here, a little blue one, take a good look at it. Make sure you can recognize it if you see it again." Without waiting for a reply, he closed the door and started the engine. He took off up Affleck Canal, flying over Kuiu Island at the head of the canal and circling wide before heading back towards Wrangell. No doubt about it, dealing with Ray was beginning to be a pain. He must have spent most of the week drinking over at Kook's Cove. Meeting with Heather would be much more pleasant, even that nerd Dwight. At least he could carry on a conversation.

* * * * *

I was in a pleasant mood as I departed Cook's Cove and sailed down Sumner Strait. The trip with Mac had worked out well and I was glad to have been able to help. I felt like I'd accomplished something for the summer. Now I was ready to head for home. Just one quick detour and I'd be southward bound.

Setting my misgivings about Anthony temporarily aside, and, I must admit, in an attempt to regain my daughter's good graces, I set a course for southern Kuiu Island and Cape Decision. I'd spend a day or two filming the area with the video camera she'd lent me. The weather was good and with any luck I should be able to get some decent footage. Cape Decision and the outside corner of the island is a fairly dramatic place, and, if the seas remained calm, I might be able to get some good close ups that would appeal to certain kayakers. Anyway, I'd do enough to at least show that I'd made a serious effort on her behalf.

As I approached lower Kuiu the winds remained light, right at that point where I debated with myself whether or not I should start the outboard, but the tide was with me and I was still making some progress so decided against it for now. I was relaxed and in no big rush. Sitting on the cockpit seat, reading the instruction manual for the camera, I became aware of the drone of an airplane passing overhead. It reminded me of Anthony, just who I didn't want to start thinking about. I grabbed my binoculars and studied the rapidly departing plane as it banked into a turn and disappeared up Affleck Canal. It looked a lot like his plane all right.

I was planning on spending the night in that vicinity anyway, looking around the protected anchorages for interesting scenery or good campsites to film before proceeding around the cape the next day, but the lure of seeing what Anthony might be up to, if that was him, helped pull me along. As I rounded the point to the canal the breeze picked up, and I slacked the sheets to take advantage of the new wind, now almost on my stern. I made good time for a little while, but soon the fickle breeze died down again and I was barely coasting along. Before I reached Kell Bay I heard the distant sound of a float plane taking off and saw it climbing skyward. Instead of retracing its path and flying back over me however, it turned the other way and quickly became a tiny speck vanishing over the distant hills.

That's just as well, I thought, I didn't really care to see that guy again. I lowered the sails and started the engine, and, hoping to spot something interesting to try the camera on, motored along close to shore. Then something happened that changed everything. As I entered Kell Bay, a small boat came out, going fast. It would have passed far outside me but altered course in my direction. He didn't slow down as he roared by and left me wallowing in his wake. I got a good look at him staring at me from behind the wheel without so much as a nod or a wave, plus I recognized the boat. It was definitely Ray Thorp.

As much as I'd been trying to keep the business of Anthony and bears and him out of my mind, this certainly aroused my suspicions. What else would he be doing out here? And if that plane that zipped in and out was indeed Anthony they probably just completed some sort of rendezvous. Since they'd both left, I decided to poke around a bit, see if I could turn up any evidence of what had gone on here. I certainly knew what I'd be looking for.

As it turned out, it took me quite a while and a bit of luck to locate it. I motored into the corner of the bay that Ray had just come from and dropped the hook. Then I launched the ding-yak and paddled ashore, scouting for any fresh footprints or signs of human activity. I didn't find any. Kell Bay, while just one of thousands in Southeast Alaska, still encompasses a lot of area, especially when you're contemplating covering its shoreline on foot. After hiking for a half hour the futility of aimlessly walking around expecting to stumble over a dead bear dawned on me. I'd have to come up with a better plan than this.

Since bears congregate around salmon streams this time of year, I decided to start there. Returning to the sailboat, I proceeded further into the bay, watching for the sort of place I'd go if hunting bears. I anchored as close as I could to the mouth of a good sized creek and paddled to the nearest convenient spot for gaining access, a little gravel beach off to one side. And here I lucked out. After packing the ding-yak up to the high-tide line, I hadn't gone more than a few paces towards the creek when I came across fresh boot prints. Following closely, I spotted where he'd stopped and shuffled around, and left a cigarette butt lying on the beach.

Picking up the occasional track, I headed upstream. As I walked a well trodden bear path, littered with frequent large piles of scat, the incident with Dwight and the bear fresh in mind, I wondered why I was packing a video camera instead of my rifle. The fact that I might be able to document a charging bear on film before it got me was little help for the apprehension I felt. The further upstream I got and the more dense the forest became, the worse I felt. When I saw a small bear wade out of the creek ahead of me and disappear into the woods on my side of the creek

I decided to head back. I hadn't seen any boot prints for quite awhile anyway. Maybe Ray hadn't come up this far or had crossed over.

Part way back I crossed the stream on a fallen log and worked my way back down the opposite side. I was relieved to break back out into the open, but disappointed not to have seen any more sign of Ray's passing. A large grass flat extended from this side of the creek to what could be another one on the far side. As I made my way through the grass I thought I could detect from the bent stalks that someone or something had passed this way recently. Then I noticed activity before me.

Ahead, three ravens were swooping and diving and calling excitedly over something. Half way to the birds, in a patch of bare mud, I almost overlooked a clear boot track of the same sort I'd followed on the beach. My heart pounding now, I hurried on. But I already knew what to expect. At my approach, the ravens noisily retreated to the nearest trees, where they continued their raucous squawking. By then I'd spotted the unnatural looking hump in the grass.

I cleared away some of the covering and looked at the dead animal. I didn't know a lot about bears but it appeared to be a big one, in the prime of life. It was much larger than the other dead one I'd stumbled across earlier this summer. And freshly killed too. I lifted one of its forelegs and let it drop. Wasn't even stiff yet. So I'd found another dead bear, killed by the same guy. Now what?

Then I remembered the camera bag strapped to my shoulder and decided to record the scene of the crime. Feeling like some sort of amateur sleuth in a cheap novel, I retraced my path to the boot print in the mud. Activating the voice recorder, I told my name and the place and the date. As I focused on the print and began filming I said, "This is the foot print I've more or less followed to the dead bear." I rolled a little more film as I walked towards the bear, probably filming much more bent over grass than necessary.

I kept my eyes on the ground, hoping to detect another print, and was glad I did because just before reaching the carcass I detected a spent shell casing. I focused the camera on it as well as I could. "Here's an empty cartridge," I said, bending over to pick it up. "30-06 caliber. About thirty feet from the dead bear." Then I pointed out the wound in the bear's back. "Here's where he was most likely shot first, and," focusing on the shattered head, "this would've been the killing shot." I used a stick to prop open the small slit on the bears hide. "This, I assume, is where the gallbladder was removed."

A quick search of the immediate vicinity turned up nothing more than one cigarette butt, which I duly recorded and pocketed with the empty cartridge. Not very professional, I thought, to be leaving this incriminating evidence lying around. But professional or not, now that the excitement of finding the bear and filming it had passed, I suddenly felt nervous. I wanted to get out of there as fast as I could. Reminding myself that it would be stupid for the shooter to return to the scene of the crime helped some, but I still made good time back to my boat.

I pulled the anchor and motored to a distant corner of the bay to spend the night. Once there, I attempted to relax and calmly ponder what to do next. True, I probably had enough evidence to seriously implicate Ray Thorp in illegally killing a bear. If I remembered right, from growing up on a diet of TV cop shows like most people my age, a spent cartridge could be linked to the rifle that fired it. Too bad I hadn't gotten a video of Ray passing me in his boat, with some identifiable scenery in the background tying him to the area.

But I didn't really care about Ray. In fact finding a bear with only its gallbladder removed so a guy could make a few bucks struck me about the same as finding one skinned so some trophy hunter could display its hide to his friends back home. Both seemed like such a waste. No, it was that smooth talking, two faced Anthony, who was beguiling my daughter, that I cared about. And I didn't have a single thing to tie him to this. I had seen him talking with Ray in a bar and get into a truck with an oriental guy, and maybe seen his plane land in the vicinity of this bear. Big deal. It didn't take a lawyer to realize that meant nothing.

The only way to implicate Anthony with what I had would be for the cops to lean on Ray hard enough for him to turn Anthony in, hoping for a lighter sentence. That seemed far from certain. If only I had evidence of him meeting with Ray near the scene of a shooting. Surely, whatever the outcome, that would stir things up enough that his plan of being partners with Heather would fall through. It shouldn't be that hard. One shot of them meeting somewhere out in the bush ought to do it. But where? With a fast boat and a plane they could be a long ways away in short order.

Then I remembered that conversation I'd overheard back at the dock. Ray had told that guy pestering him for a ride that he was going to Tebenkof Bay. On a calm evening like this, in a fast skiff, he could be there by now. Well, that settled it. Summer was only half over and it wasn't that far out of my way. I'd go up to Tebenkof and see what developed. It seemed like fate kept dealing me into this and now I'd just play out the hand.

The morning dawned clear and calm, and, anxious to take advantage of the good conditions, I got an early start. Departing Affleck Canal I encountered a large group of sea otters at the edge of the kelp. Of all the marine mammals these are undoubtedly the most photogenic and easiest to approach. Figuring even a novice like myself might get some decent footage of these friendly seeming creatures, I shut off the engine and coasted among them. After spending more time and energy in the operation than expected, I concluded that dead bears were definitely easier to film than live animals. And it occurred to me that filming two people who didn't necessarily want to be filmed might not be all that easy. Eventually I got what I thought might be a good shot of a mother otter sculling by on her back with a pup riding on her chest.

Cape Decision is open to the west, and even though the wind remained calm, a light swell continued to roll in off the open ocean and crash against the rock cliffs. I got as close as I felt was prudent and filmed the rugged headland and lighthouse, and went on up the coast another half mile. Then I ran offshore a way and turned off the engine, to drift quietly and think things over again.

My resolve of the previous evening to follow Ray in an attempt to get incriminating evidence against him and Anthony was wavering. It didn't seem as easy now as it had yesterday after stumbling across that poorly hidden bear. At this point, if I hadn't seen Ray leaving the bay, I'd turn and head south, feeling good about my little photographic side trip. But I had seen him, for sure. And Anthony, maybe. Why did I have to keep running into these guys?

The boat rose and fell rhythmically on the gentle swell as I thought it over. On a beautiful day like this it was easy to picture a group of delighted kayakers going by, their paddles flashing in the sun. And I didn't mind picturing Heather among them, or leading them. Sure, at times it could be a treacherous place but I had confidence in her judgment concerning the sea. It was her judgment in dealing with certain people that I mistrusted. That was the rub.

I wondered where she and Dwight were now. For the most part the weather had been nice, no big storms anyway, so they should've had a good trip. About now they ought to be getting back to Wrangell to catch the ferry. And meet with Anthony? Talk over plans for next year?

That was the thought that got me going. I started the engine and swung the tiller over, aiming the boat north, towards Tebenkof Bay. It might not be that easy to gather actual evidence against them, but if I could just put Anthony and Ray there together, even without getting them together on film, that would be enough for me. That would erase any lingering doubts about the affair in my own mind, and would be enough for Heather too, I hoped.

Chapter Eight

As anxious as he'd been to return to civilization, once they entered the Wrangell boat harbor, Dwight experienced a sudden, if passing urge to return to the wilds they'd just left. Experienced from the cockpit of a kayak, the din from a nearby fish processing plant and idling boat engines, mixed with the smell of diesel exhaust, and the sight of an oily sheen and garbage on the water, all combined with the general commotion of a working harbor, was almost too much. As usual, Heather continued on, apparently undisturbed by it all.

He followed her around a long float, crowded with various types of fishing vessels. Heather could no doubt identify each type and what its intended catch was at a glance, but this whole southeast Alaskan region with all its maritime occupations was still somewhat of a mystery to him. Yet, he reminded himself, he'd learned a lot on this trip, and was quietly proud of his increased strength and abilities.

Heather was already out of her kayak, standing on the gravel beach beside the boat ramp where they'd launched well over a week ago. In her short rubber boots, she waded out and caught his bow, steadying the tippy craft as he climbed out. "Glad to be back?" She asked.

"I'm not sure yet. It seems a bit overwhelming. But I think a hot shower will make up for it."

"That will be nice." She smiled. "We've got several hours before the ferry arrives. I think I'll call and see if

Anthony's home." She turned, and without another word lifted the bow of the kayak. In what had become a well rehearsed maneuver, Dwight quickly grabbed the other end and they carried the loaded craft up the beach, then returned for the other one. With their boats now safely high and dry, they headed for the nearest phone.

Dwight had mixed feelings about contacting Anthony again. On the one hand, he had received them gracefully when they'd called on their first arrival in town. And he had insisted, along with offering the use of his shower and the promise of a good meal, that they call him on their return. So far as that went, it was all fine. But two thoughts troubled Dwight. One was Heather's obvious attraction for the man, and the other was Dave's conviction that Anthony was involved in the illegal trafficking of bear parts, and was not to be trusted.

After their departure from Mac and Dave, Heather had withdrawn into an aloof, angry silence. When he'd brought up the subject of Dave's suspicions regarding Anthony she'd so thoroughly and forcefully ridiculed the idea that he quickly dropped the subject. It took two days of good weather and great kayaking in Rocky Pass before she'd regained her normal good cheer. From then on their trip had gone well, and, even though he'd thought more about it, Dwight was reluctant to reintroduce the subject for fear of spoiling things.

As for his other concern, yes, he admitted to himself, he had been somewhat jealous. But maybe he'd been overly sensitive at the time from feeling so out of place and being made fun of about running from that bear and falling like that. Now, after successfully completing what most people would consider an arduous kayaking adventure, he felt better about himself. And with his self-confidence renewed, the more he thought about it, the more he liked the idea of meeting with Anthony again. He'd engage him in conversation, draw him out a little without actually broaching the subject, then, jealousy not withstanding, he'd attempt to arrive at a logical conclusion considering Dave's allegations. Heather beamed a smile at him as he took her hand and they walked down the sidewalk.

Anthony restlessly flicked through the channels on the TV remote while considering his other options for an evening's entertainment, which, in his opinion, were severely limited in this hick town. He was about to give up hope on both accounts, when the phone rang. Gratefully, he punched the mute button and picked up the receiver on the second ring. "Hello."

"Hi. This is Heather."

"Oh Heather, great! Where are you?"

"At the phone booth by the boat harbor."

"Good. Stay right there, I'll be right down."

"We have our kayaks and stuff, and have to get on the ferry tonight."

"No problem. We'll put them in the back of the truck when I pick you up. You can come up to the house and I'll take you to the ferry when it comes in."

"Are you sure you don't mind?"

"Sure. I'm on my way."

Dwight regarded Heather as she joined him after the brief call. She looked pleased.

"What'd he say?"

"Said he'd be right down."

It didn't take long to reach Anthony's house. The main street through town consisted of about a dozen blocks, and after they'd driven half that distance they turned uphill, went a few more blocks, and pulled up beside a newer looking house with a grand view over the town and water.

"We can watch the ferry dock right out the window, then drive down to meet it," said Anthony. He led them inside. "Now, who gets the first shower? Is it ladies first?"

He offered Dwight a glass of wine as he searched the refrigerator for dinner possibilities, and Heather headed for the shower. "I assume you'll be hungry after that long trip you've been on. You might have to settle for spaghetti, though. I usually have enough ingredients on hand for that."

Dwight took a sip of his wine as he settled onto a kitchen chair. It was good wine. "Anything will be fine with me, thanks."

He had trouble shifting the conversation to the ground he intended, as Anthony pressed him for details regarding their kayak voyage and he found himself carrying on at length about it. Soon Heather joined them, looking bright and refreshed, and it was his turn for the shower. When he got back Heather was mixing a salad, a half empty wine glass at her side, and talking excitedly with Anthony.

"Have you heard the news?" She asked. "Anthony is thinking of buying some land out somewhere to serve as a base camp for the tours. Maybe even building a small lodge. He could meet people in town and fly them out. I think it could work out beautifully."

"Oh," said Dwight. His lack of enthusiasm brought the conversation to a temporary halt. "But that reminds me," he hastily added. "I wanted to ask how one goes about getting into this flying business. It seems like a good way to get around up here."

Anthony turned his attention from the sauce he was stirring. "It's not that hard. You just take flying lessons until you get your pilot's license, then, if you can afford it, buy a plane and start flying. Or try to get a job as a pilot for someone else. Of course there's additional requirements for different ratings and so on."

"I see. If you don't mind my asking, what sort of flying do you do? I somehow got the impression that your plane was more of an Alaskan version of a personal car than a business vehicle."

Anthony laughed. "That's about all I'm using it for right now. But if you're worried about my flying credentials I can assure you everything's in order and I'm qualified to fly passengers to a lodge. I've had plenty of experience in that line of business."

"No. Certainly I'm not the one to question your flying credentials or abilities. I've never even been up in a small plane before yours. Just curious is all. Did you fly people to lodges around here? I didn't see any."

"No, not here. I've only recently moved here," he continued. "Before that I lived in the Anchorage area and had numerous flying jobs around there and the more northern regions, including a rather long stint of flying fishermen and hunters to various camps and lodges."

"Why'd you quit that and move to this small place?" Asked Heather.

Anthony sighed. "I don't know if you've ever been to Anchorage or not. But it's a big city, complete with all the problems and noise and pollution and hype of any other city in the U. S. At first it was fun, but eventually I got tired of it and wanted to move somewhere a little slower paced. And to be truthful with you," he confided, "I got tired of flying all those hunters out there so they could shoot those beautiful wild animals. I got sick of all the killing and having to fly those grinning idiots and their bloody trophies back. I want to get into the business of catering to people who can appreciate the area for what it is without blasting at everything that moves."

"I know what you mean," said Dwight.

Anthony checked the simmering sauce again. "Well, it looks like this is ready, let's eat."

Later, Dwight and Heather stood leaning against the railing at the stern of the ferry, watching the lights of Wrangell disappear in the distance. Even though Heather would never admit it, her father's warning about Anthony had weighed on her mind. Now she felt more at ease. Granted, she hadn't known him long, but the more she saw of the man and talked with him, the more she liked him, and the more convinced she was that her father was mistaken.

She turned to face Dwight, who was apparently watching the ferry's wake unfold behind them with rapt attention. "So, what did you think?" She asked.

"It's been a marvelous trip."

"Yes it has. But I was wondering what you think about Anthony now that we've talked with him again."

"He's a gracious host. I certainly couldn't fault his hospitality."

"But what about what my dad said? I know you've been thinking about it."

Dwight reluctantly shifted his gaze from the ferry's wake to Heather. "I must admit I'm not overly fond of him. Something about his manner. I don't know, maybe it's just me. He seems sincere, though, and I can easily picture him doing well with tourists. I think he'd be a great asset to what you have in mind. As for your father, it all sounds too vague and implausible. I think he's jumped to the wrong conclusion."

* * * * *

On the sail up from Cape Decision I formed a tentative plan. Conserving my meager gas supply, and not wanting to crowd Ray, I took my time. I didn't have any idea how long bear gallbladders would last before spoiling, or even if they did spoil for that matter, but reasoned that Anthony would probably allow Ray several days hunting time before their next rendezvous. The weather remained fine, with a light westerly, so I made a couple of long tacks up Chatham Strait and anchored for the night about twenty five miles from the Cape, in Gedney Harbor.

The next day I delayed my departure until the morning fog cleared, then motored out of the harbor and resumed my sail up the strait. At Swaine Point I turned to starboard and crossed Explorer Basin on a beam reach. Then, catching the flood tide, I shot through a narrow pass separating the Troller Islands from Kuiu Island, and coasted into Tebenkof Bay.

My idea was, upon reaching the bay, to slowly work my way in, listening for the sound of a distant shot, or hoping for a glimpse of Ray's skiff through the binoculars. Then, once I determined his approximate location, I'd quietly lurk in the distance, avoiding any close contact. I'd simply wait until I could see him leave or observe Anthony's plane in the vicinity. And that would do it.

Unfortunately, although I'd fished out in front of Tebenkof Bay numerous times over the years, I'd never bothered to explore the bay itself, or given it much thought, and it turned out to be larger and more convoluted than I'd anticipated. Stretching twelve miles end to end by half that across, and containing dozens of islands, small bays and creek mouths, it offered someone like Ray a nearly unlimited number of hiding places.

I held to my plan at first, but after two days of lazily poking around I began to wonder if it would work. I'd sailed, drifted and paddled more or less around the perimeter of the main bay without so much as a glimpse or sound of my quarry. I avoided probing into the far reaches for fear of either missing him or Anthony completely if they happened to meet in the opposite end from where I was, or of blundering into Ray and perhaps causing him to leave the area or abort the rendezvous. So far, I'd seen plenty of wildlife, including three bears, but the only sign of humans I'd seen was a couple of trollers off in the distance up by Point Ellis, an abandoned fox farm on a small island, and one homestead on another island that appeared to be inhabited but with no one currently home.

By the third day I was becoming restless and decided to push further into the back reaches of the bay, and for no particular reason chose the northern half. From my anchorage at Step Island, near the center of the bay, I hoisted sail and worked my way north in the light summer breeze, barely making headway. Finally I rounded Point Elena where the breeze died completely and I coasted to a stop. Not wanting to make any engine noise, I unshipped the pair of oars I had along for emergencies, and, standing in the cockpit, propelled myself the short distance to a suitable anchorage among some small islands.

Here, the waters divided again, with one branch, Elena Bay, continuing north to eventually dead end after three or four miles, and the other branch veering to the east for a of couple miles to peter out in two or three different small coves. Since these waters are well sheltered and the good weather showed no sign of deteriorating any time soon, I launched the ding-yak, loaded the video camera, and set out to explore the eastern branch.

Paddling quietly, I skirted along the southern shoreline. The tide was nearly high so I hugged the beach to make myself a little less noticeable and to watch the shore for boot prints or other sign of recent human activity. Seeing nothing to indicate Ray's presence, I continued on. After a mile and a half I approached an extensive grass-flat and what appeared to be the head of the bay, but the flow of current seemed to indicate there was more to it.

As I rounded a small point, near what had appeared to be the head of the bay, a tiny channel, running between the bank and a low headland on the opposite side, was revealed. It was only about ten feet wide but fairly deep. I coasted through with the last of the flood tide and, as I paddled around a rock, a heron, emitting a series of loud, harsh croaks, erupted from the beach beside me. It was hard to tell who was more startled and my heartbeat had just barely returned to normal when the channel twisted around another bend and suddenly before me, anchored in a pool in a long, narrow tidal lagoon, was Ray's skiff.

I'd done just what I didn't want to do, blundered right into him. I sat still, attempting to regain my composure. A couple of minutes passed with no sign of Ray appearing and I began to relax. Maybe it would work out after all. If he was off hunting I'd get a quick shot of his boat here, tying him to the place, then leave undetected. I could retreat to a more distant anchorage and wait, watching for him to leave, or hopefully for Anthony to fly in.

But I didn't want him to catch me filming his boat. Fighting off the urge to immediately flee, I forced myself to sit still as I slowly drifted closer. After watching the boat and nearby shore for another couple of minutes without spotting any movement, I raised the video camera and began filming the boat. As I swung the camera from the boat to the shoreline, my worst fear materialized right in the lens. Rifle in hand, Ray stepped from his concealed position in the woods onto the beach, just fifty feet away.

"What the hell do you think you're doing?" He hollered.

He wasn't aiming at me, but his rifle was held ready, across his chest. I'd never felt more vulnerable. "Ah, just taking a few pictures," I stammered.

His gaze was steady. "Maybe I don't want anyone taking pictures of my boat."

"I guess I should've asked, but didn't see anyone around," I said.

He didn't look appeased and I got the feeling I better start talking fast. "I'm on a photography assignment," I said. Taking pictures all around Kuiu Island for some people starting up a kayak touring business."

"You didn't come around Kuiu Island in that thing. Where's your boat? And why would you want pictures of my boat?"

"Oh, it's anchored outside here a ways. And they told me to take pictures of everything I came across and they'd sort it out later. I liked the look of your boat anchored there, the way it blends in. Besides, it gets boring just filming scenery. It's nice to put in some human interest stuff. Maybe I could get a picture of you standing next to your boat. What are you doing out here, anyway? You're the first person we've run into for quite awhile," I added.

I don't think Ray placed exactly where he'd seen me before and I could practically see the wheels turning in his head as he regarded me in silence for several seconds. Finally he appeared to reach some sort of decision and relaxed slightly before speaking.

"I'm working on a salmon spawning survey on these creeks here," he said. "Just finished up. And unless you're well armed I'd suggest not going ashore here. There's lots of bears around and some of them can get pretty ornery."

"No, I don't have a gun. And I'm not about to go ashore where there's any bears," I assured him.

He slung his rifle over his shoulder and began pulling in his skiff. "Well I'm finished here and in a hurry to get going. Don't have time for any pictures."

I quietly breathed a sigh of relief. "That's fine." I said. "I'm gonna head back too. They're probably wondering what's keeping me. Maybe I'll see you around somewhere later." I back-paddled, turning the ding-yak around, and began my retreat, trying not to imagine crosshairs centered on my back.

Soon I heard his outboard start and I moved as far over to the side of the narrow channel as I could. He idled by without a backward glance, and once he cleared the channel accelerated and quickly disappeared. I breathed another, bigger sigh of relief. I'd blown it but at least hadn't gotten shot in the process. Not yet, anyway.

As I retraced my route to the sailboat, my worries increased again. Ray would pass in sight of my boat. Surely he'd recognize it from Cook's Cove and Affleck Canal. It would have to make him suspicious. And what if he stopped and checked it out and determined I was alone. Catching me in a lie would certainly increase his suspicions. Maybe I shouldn't have told him people were waiting for me, but at the time the last thing I wanted was for him to realize I was wandering around out here alone.

It didn't take much imagination to picture a person engaged in a highly criminal act doing away with someone spying on him, especially when there were no witnesses for miles. He'd easily get away with it too. If my body disappeared and the capsized ding-yak was found drifted up on a beach somewhere near my boat, nobody would give it a second thought. Accidental death due to drowning would be a quickly reached conclusion.

I continued to hug the shoreline on my return, but this time it was for a different reason. If Ray came back, I'd hit the beach and take off on foot. It wasn't a pleasant prospect, but beat the idea of presenting myself as a sitting duck again. I began to wish I'd brought my rifle along.

I paddled on with mixed feelings of relief and apprehension, but my fear of being ambushed won out. Halfway back to the boat, I coasted ashore at a typical stretch of rocky beach backed by a dense stand of spruce and hemlocks. I carried the ding-yak about thirty feet into the woods and stashed it behind a windfall. Then I paralleled the beach, staying just inside the woods and out of sight from the water until I reached a small point. Here I sat behind a screen of shoreside alders, watching and listening.

After an hour I'd seen exactly one eagle and one seagull, and had heard nothing. I retrieved my vessel and continued on, but as I neared my sailboat my fears remained. Surely Ray would have seen it. Would he pass by in his haste to get out of there, or would he stop to investigate? He'd realize there were no other boats around, and if he had stopped to investigate he'd know I was alone. He must be nervous about that dead bear he left on the grass-flat back in Kell Bay and me showing up right afterward. And I'd be willing to bet there were more carcasses around here.

Instead of heading directly back, I swung offshore and along the opposite side of a half mile long island. My boat was anchored between its far end and two other small islands. Nearing the end of the island, I scrambled ashore on its steep rock bank and dragged the ding-yak up into the brush. I figured I'd hike overland to a point where I could discreetly observe my boat for a while before approaching. The terrain was rugged, and blueberry bushes as high as my head grew thick and tangled beneath the canopy of trees. It was slow going, but eventually I worked my way to the western tip of the island. The land here dropped off sharply to the water below and would afford a good view. When I cautiously parted the last of the brush and looked out to the scene before me, I got my second big surprise of the day. My boat was gone!

I stared, dumbfounded. This I had not expected. Briefly I considered the idea that I was looking at the wrong spot, but quickly rejected the notion after a more thorough look at the anchorage. It was the spot all right. Next I considered that in my absence my boat had simply "drug" anchor. Not likely in these calm conditions, but it could have happened. The tide had turned and was ebbing now. It had been flooding when I anchored so perhaps the anchor had lost its purchase when the current changed directions. Maybe the chain had wrapped around a fluke. But I didn't think it could have gotten far, not clear out of sight. The bottom seemed uniformly shallow all around and, as was my habit when I'd be away from the boat, I'd let out lots of extra scope.

Of two things, though, I was fairly certain. One was that with my boat gone Ray wasn't down there waiting in ambush for me. And even if he did have something to do with my boat's disappearance, he wouldn't be waiting somewhere to shoot me. It just didn't make sense. And the other was that I wanted to find my boat. Throwing my earlier caution to the wind, I hurried back to the ding-yak, slid it into the water, and began paddling at a good clip.

Upon reaching the anchorage, I stopped paddling and looked around. A sudden feeling of panic swept over me as I considered that maybe my boat had merely sunk right here on the spot, and now rested quietly below me in seven fathoms of water. But that seemed even less likely than dragging anchor. She was a simple boat with no underwater through-hull fittings or shafts that could start leaking. The hull was new and tight. Of course someone could deliberately sink the boat, but they'd have to either fill it with water or cut a hole in the bottom. And if the boat was below me there was nothing I could do about it. I preferred to think it had drifted away.

I paddled closer to the island directly down current from where I had anchored and studied the kelp growing along its rocky shoreline. The kelp stalks leaned slightly, and the direction the fronds pointed indicated the current here passed around its northern end. Not wanting to waste any more time, I hurriedly propelled myself in that direction. Rounding the tip of the island, 1 anxiously gazed to the west, in hopes of seeing my boat peacefully adrift, but was disappointed to see only the empty waters of Tebenkof Bay stretching out before me. Now I had to stop and think. It wouldn't do to just go blindly paddling off, expecting to bump into my boat.

When I first anchored the tide had been flooding, but not very hard. The wind had remained calm in here so wind was not a factor. I'd set the anchor well, with the boat tending in the direction of the weak current, and let out plenty of scope. I ruled out the possibility that it could have "drug" anywhere with the incoming tide. By the time Ray would've gotten to the boat the tide had turned, so if he'd had anything to do with it disappearing, short of literally towing it away, it would have to be in the direction of the outgoing tide. The ebb current here would continue to flow in a generally southwest direction until rounding Gap Point, where it would probably tend more towards the west, across the mouth of Tebenkof Bay and out Chatham Strait.

Then why couldn't I see it? It was a clear day with excellent visibility. But I had taken a long time returning, and, sitting as low as I was, couldn't see all that far. Could it have drifted totally out of sight on the open water by now? I paddled along the western side of the island until I reached a steep bank that was open enough to offer an unobstructed view. Here I beached and climbed to a good vantage point about thirty feet above the water. Shielding my eyes with my hand against the afternoon sun like some Indian scout in an old movie, I scanned the horizon, and immediately spotted what at first glance looked like a stick poking out of the water way off in the distance. I circled my fingers in front of one eye in imitation of a telescope, which actually helped a little, and determined it just might be a small sailboat. Vowing to never travel without my binoculars again, I scrambled down the slope to my waiting craft and shoved off.

Of course as soon as I was back down on the water I lost sight of it, but the boat had appeared to be in the opening between Gap Point, on the north, and the islands directly to the south of it, so I had good bearings. I didn't hesitate to head out in hot pursuit. I just hoped I could catch up before it reached the wide open part of the bay. Those were big waters for me in this little dinghy, and it looked like it might be blowing out there.

After two miles of hard paddling I was nearly exhausted, but was cheered by the fact that I could now see my boat. I didn't dare stop to rest though, because once the boat had cleared Gap Point the current had slackened, which allowed me to catch up somewhat, but the west wind was blowing out there and the combined effects of the current and wind were now driving her more to the south, towards a cluster of rock islands and reefs. Normally I'd never consider venturing out in these conditions in the ding-yak, but this wasn't a normal occasion.

I pressed on, and of course the further out I got the rougher it became. Fortunately I didn't have to buck into it, which, considering my tired condition, would've been futile, or take the waves on my beam, which probably would've capsized me. Instead, the wind took on more of a northwesterly slant here so I took the two foot chop on my starboard quarter. The little vessel seemed to handle it OK, and I felt I'd make it as long as I kept on course and avoided broaching.

I could see the waves crashing on the nearly submerged reef just a hundred yards downwind when I finally caught up to my boat. Now for the tricky part. It was hard enough climbing out of this highly unstable little bathtub and aboard the sailboat on flat calm water, and I didn't relish the thought of attempting it while tossing around like this. But I didn't have any time to spare so didn't bother thinking about it.

The sailboat was lying more or less sideways to the wind and waves, with the anchor line visibly trailing off the bow. I made sure the bow line for the ding-yak was clear and right between my feet, then dug in with the paddle and angled towards the upwind side of the boat, so I'd land with it on my right hand side. Just before the two hulls touched I hastily stowed the paddle and grabbed the bow line in my left hand. As they came together on the next wave, I grabbed the cockpit coaming of the sailboat with my right hand and half stood and sort of rolled or flopped right into the sailboat. I quickly righted myself, surprised that I'd made it dry and unharmed, and tied the ding-yak off to the stern cleat.

For fear of entangling the anchor line in the propeller, I didn't bother with the motor, but immediately hoisted the mainsail. This pointed the bow of the boat into the wind and, once I got the sail tight and sheeted off and the flapping stopped, things suddenly seemed under control. I pushed the tiller over and the bow fell off the wind and we began making headway. With the jib rolled about half way out we were tacking right along and cleared the reef with fifty yards to spare.

Conditions weren't bad for the sailboat, in fact it was a great day for a sail, so I snubbed the ding-yak up close to my stern, where it was riding well, and kept on going, heading west for the Troller Islands. Using a small boathook, I fished the trailing anchor line out of the water and coiled it in the cockpit. I reached the end at about sixty feet. That would be just above where the line had been spliced to the anchor chain. The unraveled end appeared to have been cut off at an angle.

I figured that after leaving me, Ray must have stopped when he saw my boat. By then he'd probably realized he'd seen me in several places recently, including aboard the sailboat as he was leaving Kell Bay. It must seem like I was following him. So in order to give himself more time before I could use my radio, or maybe as some sort of a message to not mess with him, he pulled up my anchor and simply cut it off. Of course he didn't know I'd take so long getting back. Maybe he'd even towed the boat some before casting it loose, so I'd take longer reaching it.

It was a fairly clever move. No one could ever prove that he had cut the line, or, for that matter, that it had been cut with a knife. Arguably, it may have cut itself on some sharp object on the bottom. So, if it was a total coincidence that he kept bumping into me and I had no inkling of what he was up to, he hadn't really incriminated himself. Losing my anchor was not something I could report and have anyone take seriously.

Whatever his exact motives, though, I was sure that he'd cut it. And that he was now long gone. I'd definitely flushed him out of there. I had no idea where he'd go next, nor did I really care. I had enough evidence against him anyway. It was Anthony that I'd hoped to conclusively implicate, but with Ray out of the picture, I had no way of knowing where they'd meet next. I assumed they'd either be in radio contact or have a second location arranged in advance.

Either way, it made no difference. After today's adventures I'd lost all desire of continuing the hunt. I'd turn back and head south now, back on my original route. When I reached the town of Craig, I'd leave my evidence and suspicions of the bear poaching operation with the state troopers. They could deal with it as they saw fit.

The boat sailed nicely in these conditions, and didn't take my full attention. As I neared the Troller Islands, I lashed the tiller and readied my spare anchor, which I kept handy under a seat in the cockpit. It was a folding Northhill anchor, smaller than my main one had been, but would be adequate until I could pick up another larger one. The wind nearly died in the islands, and I coasted into a snug anchorage and dropped the hook without starting my outboard.

I went below and poured myself a generous shot of rum. Nothing in or on the boat appeared to have been bothered. Slumping onto the only comfortable seat, which also doubled as my bunk, I realized I was exhausted. I took a few drinks, and before I knew it was sound asleep.

Chapter Nine

I awoke feeling stiff and sore, and in no mood to do anything strenuous. Especially paddling. I'd done enough of that the day before. I should be well rested, though. To my amazement, I'd slept nearly twelve hours. I slid the hatch open and poked my head out. Fog. Certainly not unusual this time of year. Most likely it would burn off in a few hours and we'd have a nice sunny afternoon with a westerly breeze. With my lack of electronics, I wasn't about to head out and grope around in the fog if I didn't have to.

Rummaging in the food locker, I found a small canned ham I'd been saving and cooked a five egg, ham and cheese omelette. After a leisurely breakfast, I flicked through the channels on my little, hand-held VHF radio, intending to listen in on some bored fishermen' conversations. But the airwaves were silent. Then I remembered that the salmon trollers were starting their ten day closure about now and had probably all headed for town. I retired to my bunk with some reading material, and whiled away a good portion of the day.

Eventually, it began to lighten up outside. Before getting underway, I tuned in the weather station. Like I'd expected, they were calling for morning fog, with afternoon clearing and moderate west winds, which would suit my purposes just fine, but reported that a low pressure system was approaching the coast and would bring southeast winds and rain by tomorrow afternoon. I'd better get going. With luck I'd be past Cape Decision, and across Sumner Strait before the weather changed.

I hauled the ding-yak aboard, folded it up, and secured it to the foredeck. Then I made a quick inspection to insure that everything was ship-shape. As usual, the little Honda started on the third pull, but, before I got the anchor all the way up, it sputtered and died. I lowered the anchor again and attempted to restart the engine. It coughed a few times but refused to run. It sounded like a fuel problem.

I'd thought about installing a good filter with a water trap, something I could plug my portable gas tank into. Unfortunately I hadn't gotten around to it. I got out my little tool kit, removed the engine cover, unscrewed the filter, which didn't amount to much more than a simple screen, cleaned it off, and replaced it. Then I disconnected the fuel line from the engine, and, while depressing the valve in the end of the hose with an old nail, squeezed the pump to clear the line. At first what looked like a mixture of gas and water came out. When it looked like clear gas I hooked the hose back to the engine.

After numerous yanks on the starter cord the engine sputtered to life, smoothed out briefly, then coughed and died. I repeated the procedure with the fuel line, pumping out more water. Eventually I had the outboard running smoothly and got underway.

Odd, I thought, that water should turn up in the gas now. Maybe it had accumulated in the bottom of the tank over time, or I'd gotten a shot last time I filled up. Or maybe Ray had poured some in. If he had, that too would've been fairly clever. Taking just seconds to accomplish, it would slow me down considerably, and just like with the anchor line, it would be impossible to prove. I didn't dwell on the thought, though. I was tired of the whole subject.

Actually, I was still relieved that he hadn't done anything more drastic. Like shooting me.

I motored on calm waters through the Troller Islands, past the Windfall Islands, and into Chatham Strait. Though it was now late in the day and the last of the fog was clearing, the breeze didn't amount to much. At least it was in the right direction, blowing down the strait from the northwest. Wanting to save my remaining gas in case I had more urgent need for it later, I turned off the engine and hoisted sail. It was slow going, and for the first time on this trip I found myself wishing I was aboard my troller, steaming down the strait at nine knots, with the auto-pilot doing the steering.

I passed Gedney Harbor and eventually reached Port Malmesbury. It's the last truly good anchorage on the east side of lower Chatham Strait, and I briefly considered stopping there for the night. But the breeze had picked up somewhat, and with the weather expected to change for the worse tomorrow, I was intent on making as much headway now as I could.

Shortly after passing the mouth of Port Malmesbury the wind began to slacken and blow in fitful little gusts. I tried angling further offshore, looking for better sailing, but it didn't help much and my rate of progress slowed. I had hoped to make it around Cape Decision this evening, but began to doubt I'd get there before dark. Checking the mileage on the chart, I determined I'd never make it, even if I started the engine and motored the whole distance. A big ebb tide was coming up tonight, and I didn't want to be caught in the tide rips off the Cape in the dark. Reluctantly, I steered for Table Bay, a couple miles ahead.

Table Bay is not that great of an anchorage. I'd anchored there a few times when fishing the area in the past. It's OK in settled weather. The low pressure system wasn't expected to hit the coast until tomorrow afternoon. I'd get out of there at first light and around the Cape early in the morning, motoring the whole way if necessary. I should have plenty of time to get on across Sumner Strait before the weather deteriorated too badly.

A light swell rolled into the bay from the west, and the surge broke over numerous barely exposed rocks along the rugged shoreline. Since what little wind there was came from the northwest, I nosed up into the northern corner of the bay. I dropped the sails and started the engine, and circled cautiously to make sure I wasn't too close to any rocks. Satisfied with my location, I lowered the anchor. It seemed to grab OK, so I went below to cook dinner and settle in for the night.

I awoke sometime during the night to the rhythmic rise and fall of the boat in a building swell. I'd been dreaming that I was heading out to sea, lying in the bunk of an old fishing schooner. It was still dark and I was reluctant to get up. Listening intently for sounds of wind, I determined it wasn't blowing enough to matter and told myself to go back to sleep. Dawn would arrive in a few hours and I'd take stock of the situation when I could see.

I dozed off for a while, but the next time I woke up there was no doubt. I'd have to get up. Wind was whistling through the rigging and the boat was now pitching and bucking, and tugging at its anchor line. Obviously the bad weather had moved in sooner than anticipated.

In all the years I'd listened to the marine weather forecasts, probably seventy five percent of the time they overestimated the strength of the arriving storms, and underestimated the amount of time it would take for them to arrive, no doubt wishing to err on the side of safety. Every once in a while they'd err the other way though, and this was one of those times. The low pressure system offshore must have suddenly intensified and hit the fast track for the coast.

I pulled on my pants and rubber boots, wool coat and watch cap, and slid open the hatch. It was a dark night. Although not raining yet, the moon and stars were obscured by heavy cloud cover. The wind blew from the south, the worst possible direction for this anchorage. It would be light enough to see in another hour or so, and I considered trying to hold on where I was until dawn. I really wished I was aboard my troller now.

It would be so easy. With a powerful and reliable diesel engine purring beneath my feet, I'd be in a nice warm wheelhouse, surrounded by the faint glow of my electronic screens pinpointing my exact position. I'd engage the hydraulic anchor winch and, guided by the radar, motor right out of there. Sure, I might take a little water over the bow, but not enough to matter. I'd done that very thing a dozen times in many different locations. Nothing more than a routine anchor drill when the wind shifts or kicks up during the night.

A sharp gust of wind jerked me back to my present reality and made the decision about waiting for daylight for me. As the boat heeled over and veered to the side, the small anchor lost its grip and I felt it begin dragging over the rocky bottom. No use trying to hang on here any longer. A gale was coming up and I was against a lee shore. Dark or not, I had to get out of there.

Hurriedly, I cranked on the outboard. It started right up and ran smoothly. Before putting it in gear, I dashed up to the bow and, balancing on the plunging foredeck, pulled up the anchor. In these conditions it wouldn't do to have any loose lines or gear, so I took the time to lash the anchor firmly in place. I could just make out the dark form of the shoreline as I shifted to forward and began creeping ahead.

I made it to the midpoint of the bay with no trouble, but here I encountered the full force of the wind and seas. And this was no mere wind-chop, like in Tebenkof Bay. These waves were muscular brutes, charging in unfettered from the North Pacific Ocean. I turned now and headed directly out. Behind me I could discern the dark landmass rising behind the bay and hear the surf crashing on the beach much closer than I liked. In front of me lay the open waters of Chatham Strait. All I had to do now was keep her bow into the wind and waves, and buck my way out for at least one mile. Two would be better. Then I could turn and run for the shelter of Port Malmesbury.

I'd never been in seas this large in the sailboat before. Each and every wave we climbed up and over was a memorable occasion. The little motor would lug down and struggle as we fought our way up, then rev up as we plunged over the crest and into the trough. But we were making headway. I was nervous, but confident we'd get out of there if conditions didn't worsen.

Then it happened. As we fought our way over a particularly large, steep wave, the motor began to run ragged, then coughed and died. Instantly the boat was turned sideways to the wave and shoved back towards the beach. There must have been a little more water in the bottom of the tank, and all this pitching about had just brought it into contact with the fuel pickup. Frantically, I pulled on the starter rope to no avail.

I considered my options. Drop the anchor? No, it was too rough and would never hold. Besides I didn't even want to think about crawling out to the bow and struggling to get it overboard. Hoist the sails? Maybe if they were perfectly reefed and trimmed, and I had lots of room,

I could sail in these conditions. But I seriously doubted my abilities to sail out of this classic, sailboat nightmare of being trapped in a rising gale on a lee shore. I'd have to clear the gas line.

I needed something small and pointed to hold the valve open while I pumped the water and gas through the line. I patted my pockets. Nothing on me. I hated to risk opening the hatch for fear of half filling the cabin with water if a wave caught us wrong, but had no choice. Hanging on until the next crest passed beneath, I opened the hatch, stuck my arm in, and groped blindly on a little catch-all shelf just inside the cabin. My hand located a small phillips screwdriver. That would do.

I closed the hatch just as another wave laid the boat over, nearly on its side. Once the boat had righted itself, I quickly disconnected the fuel line, and wedged myself down on the floor of the cockpit. Clearing the line took both hands, one to squeeze the pump and the other to jam the screwdriver into the end of the gas hose. Lying sideways to the waves, we rolled to such an extent that I had to repeatedly let go with one hand or the other and grab onto the boat to prevent being tossed overboard. All the while we were being relentlessly driven towards the beach.

It was too dark to tell what exactly was coming out of the fuel line, but eventually I felt I'd pumped enough liquid through it to give the engine a try. Timing my moves with the roll of the boat, I got the line connected and began yanking on the starter cord. It started on about the tenth pull.

I jammed the outboard into forward and increased the speed. Just as I swung the tiller over to point us offshore, I heard a roar and looked up to see a large breaker dead ahead. Before I could react it picked us up and slammed the boat down on its port side. There was a sick-

ening crash and the sound of wood splintering as we landed on a rock. We bounced once and were over the rock,
on the inshore side. Miraculously I'd managed to stay
aboard and the engine still ran. But I knew the boat was
lost.

There was only one thing to do. With no plan in
mind now other than to avoid drowning, I cranked the throttle to full speed and aimed us directly towards the beach.
We surged forward on the following waves and, before I
knew it, were into the crashing surf. Luckily we hit at a
steep rock beach instead of a sheer cliff. The keel struck
and the boat slewed around to starboard, laying over on its
already damaged and lower port side.

The force of the impact broke the backstay, and I
had a glimpse of a swinging boom and toppling rigging
before a wave broke over the stern and I was sent flying
into a smother of foam. I tumbled around and had just
barely figured out which way was up and gotten a breath
of air, when another wave broke over me and I surged up
the beach. The water retreated and I got a firm grip on a
boulder as the backwash pulled against me. When the
seaward suction slackened, I scrambled up the beach and
out of reach of further waves.

I sat down and regained my breath. When I'd been
in the water I hadn't even noticed the cold. Now I shiv-
ered uncontrollably. I realized it was pouring down rain.
Not that I could get any wetter, but it certainly wouldn't
help me warm up. I'd have to start moving. It was still too
dark to see well, but it looked like the boat was engulfed in
surf about half the time, so there was nothing I could do
there now. Fortunately the tide would be going down for
another hour or two. Maybe I could salvage something
later.

I made my way up to the high tide line and stumbled around in the dim light. I took off my coat and tried to wring it out, and passed the time alternating between jumping jacks and running in place. Eventually the shivering slowed, but I never did get warm. When it was light enough to see what I was doing, I picked my way down to what was left of my beached boat.

The bow of the boat faced inland and was relatively undamaged. I felt a surge of relief when I noticed the ding-yak lashed in place, unharmed. Feeling cold and slow and clumsy, I untied it and carried it up the beach. The broken mast and a tangle of rigging and the main sail lay beside the boat. I got most of the sail pulled loose from the wreckage and cut it away with my pocket knife.

With its stern just beyond the reach of the breakers below, the boat rested precariously on the steep beach. Abaft the mast, the whole port side was completely stove in. I approached the stern cautiously. The hatch was torn off and I looked inside. Total wreckage. I stood there, in the lashing rain and gale force wind, staring at it for a long time. My mind felt like it was working in slow motion. Finally, I had to consciously tell myself to get moving. In my dazed condition, I could see nothing inside worth crawling in for. Just inside the hatchway was a plastic container with its lid still on. I knew it contained rice, and took it. Somehow, in the cockpit, were three cans of food. I gathered them up too.

On the way back up to where I'd stashed the sail and ding-yak, I spotted a red object fifty yards down the beach. My gas can. I hurried after it. Now I knew I'd survive if I did things right. In one end-compartment of the dinghy I had a little beach kit, which included some matches in a watertight container, a hatchet, a small aluminum pan, a few food bars, and some tea, all stored away in case I wanted a shoreside picnic someday.

Fuel would be no problem. I was on a small point of land that jutted out near the center of Table Bay. In testimony of the severe storms that often lashed the area, it was covered with driftwood. I portaged my meager supplies over the jumbled logs in search of a sheltered spot to set up camp. I found a place just beyond the last of the driftwood and behind a giant rock that had a few stunted, twisted trees growing off it, and was separated from the main hillside by fifteen feet of fairly level ground.

It was a relief to be out of the wind. I put the gas can on the ground, then sat down on it. After a time I realized I was just sitting and staring, and once again had to consciously tell myself to get moving. I started gathering wood. Finding a piece of drift cedar that felt fairly light, I got out the hatchet and split off a bunch of kindling. When I was sure I'd accumulated enough wood to last a while, I arranged a stack of kindling, poured a generous splash of gas on it, struck two matches together, and tossed them on the pile.

The fire roared to life. I added more split cedar, gradually working up to bigger and bigger pieces until I had a good blaze going. I added some larger chunks and hunkered as close as I could without burning myself. Despite the heavy rain, steam rose from my clothes and I finally began to warm up, one side at a time.

Eventually, I gained enough energy to get busy again. I filled my pan with fresh water from a nearby rivulet and set it at the edge of the fire. Now I needed shelter from the rain. I dragged the sail over, and using scraps of line and a pole from the driftwood pile, rigged a makeshift tent. It was a crude little affair, but kept the rain off. I had the open end facing the fire, which was backed by the rock, so some of the heat was reflected into the tent.

I brewed some tea and, while waiting for it to cool,

ate one of my food bars. I didn't wait long enough for the tea to cool, and burned my mouth on the edge of the pan, but the scalding liquid finally warmed my insides. Suddenly, I was overcome with exhaustion. The tent hadn't used all of the sail material, so I cut a large piece off and held it in front of the fire to warm it up. When it was dry and toasty, I wrapped myself in it, laid down in the tent, and fell into a deep sleep.

Since I didn't have a watch, I didn't know what time it was when I woke up, but it must have been late afternoon. The fire was down to ashes and a few coals. I felt stiff and sore, and looked myself over. One pant leg was ripped at the knee and my leg was a little scraped and bruised. That and a few superficial scratches on my hands, probably from the barnacles on the boulder I'd clung to, were the extent of my bodily damages. Physically, I'd come through the wreck in good shape.

The rain had let up, but I could still hear the wind in the trees and the crashing surf. I gathered more wood and revived the fire, then went to see if there was anything left of my boat.

Where the boat had struck, I could see nothing but a mass of white water pounding the beach. With my head bent into the wind, I patrolled the high tide line and found part of the broken mast, the ruined hatch cover, a two foot section of plywood deck, and a few miscellaneous scraps of wood. That was it. The boat had been demolished. Probably the lead keel and a few attached pieces of the hull were still underwater.

Oddly enough, what struck me as sad as I surveyed the desolate scene of the wreck was not so much that I had lost the boat, but that it had ended its short life, lost at sea, without having been named or properly christened.

During the construction, and in fact right up to the

time of my departure, I'd toyed with various names, but never came up with one that satisfied me. I'd rejected using the name of my wife or daughter, and was now glad of that. Maybe even back then I'd sensed it wouldn't be with me long enough to name after one or the other of the two most important people in my life. But I could have named it something. Trouble was, all the names I thought of that seemed fitting for the boat, like *Feather Wind* or *Autumn Breeze*, or some such thing, also seemed too flowery, or whimsical, or trite. Now it had gone to an early grave, unnamed.

Oh well, I chuckled to myself. I should've named it the *Chatham Strait*, since that's where it ended up. Making my way back to camp, I almost stepped on my blue watchcap, nearly buried in a pile of popweed and kelp. I wrung it out and stuck it on my head.

Back at the fire, I took stock of my larder. I had three food bars, not much more than glorified candy bars really, a quart of rice, and a can each of corn, chili, and peaches. I selected the chili, and, using the corner of my hatchet blade, eventually got it opened. While it was warming, I carved out a little wooden spoon with my pocket knife.

Making do, as I was, got me thinking about all the things I wished I could have salvaged off the boat. Numerous items would've made my situation easier, but the one I regretted losing the most was Heather's video camera. The camera, of course, could be easily replaced. It was actually the film and evidence against Ray, and maybe Anthony, that I really hated losing, not to mention all the footage I'd shot for Heather along the way. Without that, the whole trip over here, and consequent loss of the boat, seemed so pointless.

I ate my chili, and stared at the fire and moped. I went over the chain of events that put me here, and a long list of "I should haves", and "if onlys". I tried to blame Ray for the whole thing, but knew my own poor seamanship was mostly responsible.

Eventually, the dark thoughts ran their course, and I realized that even though I was temporarily safe and sound, I was still in a tricky situation and would need a clear head to get myself out. I began making plans.

Chapter Ten

As is usually the case in summer, the storm quickly blew itself out. By noon of my second day in Table Bay, the weather had settled into a gray, drizzly stillness. Of course, a large swell, left over from the gale, continued to roll in and break against the beach, but it was rapidly losing force. If the wind remained calm, I'd probably be able to risk launching the ding-yak tomorrow.

I figured there was no point in staying where I was any longer than necessary. Once the trolling season opened back up, and if someone happened to stumble onto fish nearby, a boat or two could possibly anchor in the bay. But it was nothing I could depend on. A whole year could just as easily pass before another boat came in here. And since I'd been calling my wife on a fairly sporadic basis, she wouldn't report me overdue or missing for at least a couple more weeks. So a search wouldn't get underway for me for a long time. Furthermore, I wasn't in the mood to sit around waiting to be rescued anyway.

Due to the rugged terrain and lack of human habitation in the area, there was no point in attempting to get anywhere overland. That left me with the option of paddling out of there in my dinghy, which I'd attempt as soon as conditions allowed. In the meantime, I made preparations.

Even though I was marooned on what was essentially a wilderness beach, a surprising amount of man made garbage had accumulated. Plastic containers were the most numerous, and just what I needed. First off, I found an empty one gallon bleach container to serve as a fresh water jug. Then I probed the drift until I located an old detergent squeeze bottle. Since room in the ding-yak was severely limited, I could never hope to bring my gas can. The squeeze bottle, full of gas, would be a convenient fire starter. Another gallon jug with the bottom cut off would serve as an effective bailer, something I hoped I wouldn't need.

At low tide, I scoured the rocks for shellfish to augment my food supply. Aboard the ding-yak, I had a small handline and a few fishing lures. Once out on the water, I knew I could catch all the fish I'd need, but the chances for success from the beach were few, and the chances of losing gear were great. I pried several dozen quarter-sized limpets off the rocks with the tip of my knife blade. For now, I'd settle for these.

While my pot of rice cooked, I scooped the tiny meats from the limpets. When the rice was almost done, I added the meat and the can of corn. It wasn't bad. And I had enough left over for breakfast.

The next morning dawned still and gray, and the surf was down. Perfect. I wolfed down my breakfast and began dismantling camp. In a way, I almost hated to leave. While I didn't think much of the overall location, my little campsite was snug and comfortable. Last night I'd gathered up a thick mattress of moss and had slept well. Nonetheless, I didn't tarry.

Before leaving, I looked around to make sure I wasn't forgetting anything. I didn't have much to worry about. I had the clothes I wore, which consisted of a pair of socks and rubber boots, a pair of boxer shorts and black cotton work jeans, a tee shirt, a flannel shirt, and a wool coat and hat. Besides that, I had the two pieces of sail and some old rope, my beach kit and fishing line, my three plastic containers, one can of peaches, and the rice. My coat pocket held the two remaining food bars. I patted my pants pocket to make sure my knife was still there, and was ready to go.

From a distance the sea had looked flat. Now, standing right at its edge, I realized the gentle surge rolling in was a little bigger than I'd thought, not enough to be life threatening, but big enough to capsize me if I did it wrong. Hoping to stay dry, I took my time and located a good launching spot. Then I stowed the gear in the ding-yak, arranging the sail pieces as a seat cushion and back rest. When everything was ready, I timed my launch to coincide with the smallest looking set of waves and shoved off. A half dozen strokes with the paddle and I was out of harm's way. Except for taking in a little water in one boot, the launch had been perfect.

Although I had a dangerous stretch of water to cover in a very small, unseaworthy craft, my spirits soared as I paddled out the bay. I had no intention of attempting to round Cape Decision. I'd leave that to the real kayakers, with their larger, decked over, spray skirted boats, and Eskimo rolling abilities. The sooner I got out of these ocean swells, the better. I proceeded with no definite plan in mind except to head for more sheltered waters. Other than that, I'd take things as they came.

In Chatham Strait a lazy three foot swell rolled placidly in from the southwest. Out here it didn't really bother me. As long as the wind didn't come up and I didn't have to attempt a landing along the rocky, exposed shoreline, I'd be fine. According to my rough calculations, the tide should be flooding for a few more hours. Port Malmesbury lay six or eight miles ahead. Hopefully I could make it before the tide turned.

With the help of the current, I followed the Kuiu Island shore, staying out just far enough to avoid any breaking swells on offshore rocks. In time, my anxieties about being here diminished, while my spirits continued to soar. Actually, it kind of surprised me. Part of my mind tried to tell me that I should be sad, overcome with grief about losing the boat that I'd put so much work into recently. But that's not the way I felt. I felt good.

The feeling reminded me of an episode in my life many years ago. I was in my early twenties, and on a road trip from Washington State to Wisconsin, chasing down a girlfriend. The car I was driving, an old '59 Ford, was a lemon, and, despite all the work and money I'd put into it, continued to plague me with breakdowns. When it failed to start in the parking lot of a Safeway, in a small town in Idaho, I simply abandoned it. Stuffing my belongings into an old duffle bag, I walked out to the highway and, with feelings of high spirits and adventure, stuck out my thumb. I made it to Wisconsin in little more time than it would've taken me to drive, and spent a lot less money in the process. I never did regret leaving that car.

Rising and falling hypnotically on the gentle swell, with no sound other than my breathing and the hiss of surf on the nearby shore, I paddled on, lost in my thoughts. I reached the entrance to Port Malmesbury sooner than I expected. Originally, I thought I'd be doing good to get this far today. But now, with such favorable conditions, I decided to press on. Getting beyond the two mile wide mouth of the inlet this morning would be a significant accomplishment. Once I passed Point Harris, on the inlet's opposite side, only a few miles remained before reaching Gedney Harbor and a stretch of sheltered waters.

I'd been trolling a salmon lure for the last hour without so much as a nibble, and had nearly forgotten about it when, just off Point Harris, a jerk on the line startled me. For lack of a better place, I'd secured the line around my left leg, and could now feel the steady pulse of a good sized fish. Since getting a lively salmon aboard this tiny craft could be tricky, I decided to tow it along for a while, hoping it was well hooked and would stay on the line.

After fifteen minutes the jerking subsided to a steady drag, so, hand over hand, I began pulling it in. Twenty feet from the boat, the fish came to life again. I wrapped the line around my leg and resumed paddling. The salmon jumped and thrashed wildly, but soon tired. When it had given up the fight, I quickly brought it alongside. Shifting my weight slightly to lower one gunwale, I held my breath and slid the ten pound coho aboard.

Once the excitement of catching my dinner wore off, I realized how hungry and tired I was. If I remembered correctly, Harris Cove lay just a mile or two ahead. That would be the next available good landing spot. Though the swells had diminished in size up here, the tide was now turning and the current running against the waves would cause them to bunch up and become steeper. Hugging the shoreline in hopes of encountering less current, I pressed on.

Gratefully, I rounded the corner into Harris Cove. The last half mile had been a struggle against the increasing flow of the ebb tide. The cove is open to a west wind, and its entrance is guarded by numerous rocks. Since there are much better anchorages for larger boats nearby, I'd never been in here before. I paddled its southern shoreline, looking for a good campsite. As I neared the end of the bay, I followed a narrow passage around an island and entered a beautiful, completely protected back bay.

Spying a nice gravel beach on the inner side of the island, which was backed by red huckleberry bushes, I grounded the ding-yak, stiffly clambered ashore, and began gorging on the ripe berries. Once I'd eaten my fill, I walked back and forth on the beach, working the kinks out of my legs, and feeling pleased with myself.

I'd covered ten or twelve miles of potentially rough and dangerous water today, and was now at an excellent campsite. Firewood, while not as plentiful as at Table Bay, was available. My jug of water was nearly full, and I had more food than I could eat, including berries behind me, beach greens at my feet, and a nice fresh salmon. Plus, the sky was clearing. What more could I ask for?

The next thing I did was find a suitable location and put up my makeshift tent. Even though the day was warming and I now had my coat off for the first time since the wreck, I didn't completely trust the rain to hold off. Once my shelter was finished and a moss bed arranged, I turned my attention to getting a fire going and some more food in me. When the fire was under control, I splashed a little water into my pan and laid a chunk of fish in it. Soon enough, I had a nice piece of poached salmon.

After lunch I built the fire back up and took the hatchet in search of green alders. Probing a tangle of the twisted, shrub-like trees, I located one about two inches in diameter with a suitable fork, and cut it down. Back at the campsite, I trimmed it and wove some smaller branches through the fork in an attempt to make a cooking rack. I filleted the salmon and eventually got the pieces lashed onto my crude holder. Using a log and a couple of big rocks, I propped the affair up so the fish leaned well above the fire.

In hopes of keeping away the biting insects, which were coming out now, and to give the fish a smoke flavor, I piled the green alder trimmings on the fire. Reclining on the beach, just under the billowing smoke, I scrunched into the gravel and made myself comfortable. Soon I dozed off.

The smell of cooking salmon and the sizzle of fat as it dripped off the fish and onto the fire woke me. I spent the rest of the afternoon slowly cooking the fish, and alternating between tending the fire and napping. When the fish was done to perfection and just about to flake apart on its own, I set it aside to cool and put a pot of water on the fire.

Starting at the high tide line, the whole beach along here was covered with a three inch high plant that the locals call beach asparagus. Unless soaked for a long time first, it's too salty and not really that tasty, but thinking it might be good for me, I gathered a few handfuls and threw them in the pot. Taking my time, I feasted on the salmon, which was delicious, and managed to eat most of the greens. I sat by the fire until dusk, then wrapped myself in my piece of sail and went to bed.

Sometime in the middle of the night, at the conclusion of a dream, I woke up. As far as dreams go, it didn't seem like much. It was very brief and concise. The striking thing was how clear and vivid it had been, one of those dreams that seem more real than being awake.

I'd simply dreamed that I was in a brightly colored advertisement, declaring sailboats as the ultimate escape to paradise. Leave your troubles and worries behind and sail away to tropical splendor and bliss. In the dream, I was in the ad, in fact, somehow, I was the ad, but even though I was doing it, I didn't really believe it. I woke up feeling troubled, and pondered the dream awhile before drifting back to sleep.

Another peaceful day greeted me in the morning. I ate my second to the last food bar and packed up, but, since the tide is roughly an hour later each day, I had some time to kill before it would begin flooding. I wasn't in a big enough hurry to waste my energy bucking the current.

Yesterday, when tired from paddling kayak style, I would take my two-piece paddle apart and use one half, canoe style. The trouble was the metal socket on the end was hard on my hand. While waiting for the tide to turn, I found a suitable piece of driftwood and carved a handle to fit snugly into the socket. When it looked like the water level in the bay was no longer dropping, I launched and headed out.

The weather remained overcast but calm, and the surge this far up the strait was almost nonexistent. I set off following the shoreline, skirting offshore boulders and kelp patches. Conditions this morning didn't feel as threatening as they had yesterday, and I wasn't nearly as keyed up as I had been. As if on auto-pilot, I paddled methodically, paying little attention to my surroundings. I was lost in thoughts concerning my dream.

Usually by the following morning, any memory I retain of a dream is nothing more than sketchy flashes of a vague and convoluted series of distorted images. But this dream was so short and simple, and had come through so clearly, I couldn't get it out of my mind. I thought it must be important somehow. At first it didn't seem to make any sense. I'd never had any intentions of sailing away to a tropical paradise. I merely wanted to take a closer look at an area I was already familiar with. As I thought it over though, it slowly dawned on me.

It would be hard to deny that sailboats often represent a vehicle for escaping one's present circumstances or location. A glance at any cruising publication would quickly confirm this. I, too, had been using my sailboat for just that. True, I'd known all along that I wanted to escape the demands of an often hectic and rigorous fishing season, at least for one year. More importantly however, with the help of Heather's recent comments, I now realized I'd also been unconsciously using the sailboat, especially in the planning and building phases, to escape my home circumstances.

About the time I conceived of the project and started on it, my relationship with my wife was beginning a long, gradual, downhill slide. It was nothing dramatic, like wild fights or emotional confrontations, just a slowly widening gulf opening between us. When Heather, our only child, left home, Karen was left feeling somewhat empty and unfulfilled. She turned to me for increased companionship and reassurance. Not being very good at offering such things, I responded in a casual and shallow manner.

The more she wanted from me, the more aloof I became. I'd no sooner get back from fishing and then it was time to go on the annual elk hunt with the guys. Then I immersed myself in the sailboat project and spent all my time studying boat designs, and lofting and building the boat. When I wasn't actually out in the shop working, I sat around daydreaming about it, withdrawing more and more into my sailing fantasies, and ignoring Karen's hints for attention and a dream we could share. For diversion, I'd go down to the coffee shop at the dock and B.S. with the other fishermen.

Heather was right. It was no wonder Karen gave up on me and left. I may have supplied a yearly income, but was offering almost nothing of myself. I just hoped she hadn't given up on me for good.

One thing was certain though. I knew I'd never bother to replace my sailboat. Sailing was OK, and even fun at times, but I hadn't really been looking forward to the return trip to Washington. In fact, I realized now that I'd even been dreading it a little. For better or for worse, this was one sailboat escape that was definitely over.

Five miles off shore a huge, white cruise ship caught my eye and pulled me out of my reverie. I stopped paddling and watched it pass. Once in Sitka, I'd briefly spoken with a couple off one of these luxury liners. They said that, with the extravagant meals and constant supply of fresh pastries and snacks, the main challenge on the tour was to avoid gaining too much weight. The difference of circumstances between those passengers and myself right now could hardly be greater. And while my current situation would be considered dire by many, I didn't really long to join them. For that matter, I didn't have any way of attracting the ship's attention even if I wanted to. But I sure would've liked some of their excess food about now.

At twenty knots, the cruise ship quickly receded, and lingering thoughts of fresh baked pastries reminded me of my gnawing hunger. I lowered my fishing line and resumed paddling. Rounding Point Cosmos and approaching Gedney Harbor, numerous humpback salmon jumped around me. As usual, they were biting on pink or red colored lures and I hooked and lost two of the frisky little things before I managed to boat one. It only weighed three or four pounds but would make a good lunch.

I paddled into the protected waters of Gedney Harbor. Until just a few years ago, a fish buying barge had anchored here for the duration of the season, servicing the local troll fleet. The company had discontinued the operation due to decreasing profits, so now anyone fishing the area had to run their fish over to Port Alexander, across Chatham Strait. While I normally fished further offshore, I remembered coming in here to unload one time in the late 1970's.

I'd been amazed at the size of the rag-tag fleet and all the hippie handtrollers in the area. Probably a dozen camps lined the shore ranging from a genuine Indian tee-pee to the crudest of visqueen shelters. The occupants fished the nearby waters in a variety of craft, most little more than small open skiffs, including one large dory that looked like it had migrated directly from the Grand Banks off Nova Scotia. They sold their catch daily and the fish buyer supplied them with gas and groceries and other essentials. It looked like fun.

That fleet had dwindled out over the years though, the fishermen either quitting or moving up to larger boats, much as I had done. Only I hadn't started off so small to begin with. Now the harbor lay deserted and I had the whole place to myself.

In the area where I remembered seeing most of the camps, a gentle gravel beach lined the inside of the island which protected the harbor. I paddled ashore and, with the usual grunts and groans, disembarked and stretched. Spending more than two or three hours at a time crammed into the ding-yak was fairly torturous and, even though the tide was still flooding, I was happy to stop. Thankfully, now that I was out of the swells, I could pretty much land whenever I felt like it.

I walked around, eating blueberries and exploring the old campsites. I didn't find much. In this climate anything left lying around either quickly rots away or gets covered by brush. Then, just as I was about to turn back, I stumbled across two grates beside an old campfire ring. They were just a couple small racks out of a refrigerator or something, but would make cooking over a fire much easier. Clutching my new-found treasure, I hurried back to my supplies.

Once wood was gathered and the fire was going, I arranged a beach stone at either end of the flames. Then I put a rack across the stones and placed the humpie fillets on it. When the fish was about half cooked, I put the other rack on top and, using my coat sleeves as pot holders, turned the whole thing over. It was a vast improvement over the forked stick method. I devoured the whole fish, then packed up and shoved off.

Detouring over to a small stream, I filled my water jug, then continued on. I followed the inside of the island and worked my way through a patch of rocks at its northern end. Gliding over the bottom only two feet below me, I worked my way around more kelp patches and rocks and inside a line of small islands. The tide was ebbing now, but by staying right at the edge of the kelp which lined the beach, I was able to pick up a few back eddies and avoid most of the current.

I covered another two or three miles that way and reached Swaine Point, where I went ashore to stretch and rest. I calculated I'd made eight or ten miles so far today, and figured, all things considered, I was doing pretty good. I imagined that Heather could easily cover three times that distance in her kayak.

The point was not an attractive campsite and I didn't intend to spend the night there. I'd wait until the tide changed, then, catching a little of the evening flood, press on again. While waiting, I searched the rocks for seafood. Clam beaches abounded in the area and I could have easily dug my fill, but was afraid to eat them for fear of red tide. I had no desire to survive a shipwreck and cover miles of treacherous waters in a minuscule dinghy, only to be done in by poisonous clams.

Sometimes during the summer, clams become contaminated with paralytic shellfish poisoning, commonly called red tide, which can be deadly to humans. I knew that the local Indians didn't eat clams in the time between the spawning of herring and the spawning of salmon, which roughly corresponds with the old white man's saying of don't eat shellfish in a month without an R in it. I also knew that abalone and limpets weren't affected, and that Indians sometimes gathered a thumb-sized creature, which they called "gum boots", off the rocks during the summer.

I filled my bailer with a collection of some good-sized limpets, several creatures resembling shell backed slugs, which I was pretty sure were "gum boots", and one small abalone. I had to take off my coat and shirt and immerse my arms up to the shoulders to get the abalone, but it was my prize catch. When the current let up, I pushed off and paddled a couple miles across Explorer Basin to a nice little beach on one of the Windfall Islands. There I made camp and prepared dinner.

From the texture of the meat, it quickly became apparent how "gum boots" got their name. So, utilizing a piece of flat driftwood for a table, I lined up all the shelled meats, including the abalone, and beat on them with the edge of a narrow rock. After the tenderizing process, I cut it all into bite sized pieces and cooked up another rice and shellfish stew. I'd worked up enough of an appetite that it tasted good.

After dinner I considered opening my can of peaches for dessert, but decided to wait another day. At my present rate, I figured I had enough fire starter, matches and rice to last three more days. After that, things would start to get a bit bleak. Of course if I limited myself to one fire a day, the matches and gas would last twice as long. I could also get a fire going without the gas but, in this damp weather, would undoubtedly use many more matches in the process. It was time to develop a plan.

I could paddle over to the homestead I'd seen earlier, but then what? If they were still gone, I could make myself at home until they arrived, I supposed. Or if they were there, they could give me a ride over to Port Alexander or somewhere, or maybe call a plane to pick me up. Neither of those ideas appealed to me though. I guess I didn't feel desperate enough yet to go knock on a stranger's door, asking to be rescued. Or maybe I was just too vain.

That left me with only two options. Stay put, or keep going. No point in staying where I was, except that at least I was safe here. As long as the weather remained calm, though, I might as well keep heading up Chatham Strait. Once the troll season opened back up, sooner or later I'd bump into someone. Most likely it would be a fisherman out of Kake, and I could catch a ride back to town with him. For that matter, I could probably make it there on my own, but it was a long way and I didn't relish the idea of all that work. After only two days of paddling, I was already tired of it. I hoped Heather's future clients had a better attitude than mine.

As I sat there mulling it over, a new idea popped into my head. A portage; I could make a portage. I remembered from looking at the charts that the next bay up from Tebenkof, called Bay of Pillars, nearly reached another which extended over from the northern end of Rocky Pass. If my memory was correct, not more than a half mile of land separated the two bodies of water. Weather permitting, I could easily reach Bay of Pillars tomorrow. I'd paddle to its end, carry the ding-yak across, hopefully it wouldn't be too steep or brushy, and continue on.

From there it would be easy. All I had to do was turn right at the mouth of the bay and I'd be in Rocky Pass. I'd catch the current and coast right through, then paddle over to Mac's floathouse. If all went well, it shouldn't take more than a total of three days to get there. If the ten day fishing closure had started on the day of my shipwreck, then Mac might be home when I arrived. If not, I'd make myself comfortable, rest up, and eat some of his food. Then maybe I'd borrow his outboard skiff and buzz over to Cook's Cove.

Once again, reaching Mac's floathouse in Three Mile Arm had become a destination for me. Feeling eager about getting on with my journey, I drifted into a restless slumber.

Chapter Eleven

As the bow of the ding-yak knifed through an opening between patches of kelp, masses of the undulating seaweed on either side of me rose and fell in time with the low swells. The lane of open water was scarcely wider than the little boat, and, in order to avoid dragging the paddle blades through the heavy kelp, I maneuvered through using just half of the paddle, canoe style.

Steep and battered looking, Point Ellis rose just off my starboard side, and shallow water and offshore rocks covered by kelp extended to my port. Despite the forbidding nature of the place, I was glad to be here. In just a few more minutes I'd round the point and put Chatham Strait behind me. I'd taken a risk this morning and had been nervous for the last two hours.

Waking early, and anxious to be on my way, I'd broken camp and had departed Windfall Islands at the crack of dawn. My original idea had been to cut through the Troller Islands and across Tebenkof Bay to the nearest point on the Kuiu shore. Then I'd follow the shoreline to Point Ellis. That way, once I covered the two mile stretch across the bay, I could stay within a stone's throw of the beach up to and around the point.

The trouble with that route was that it was considerably longer than a straight line to Point Ellis. A few minutes out of camp I paused to reconsider. Ever since the storm, the weather had remained peaceful; low overcast, off and on drizzle, and almost no wind, perfect for travelling. The morning ebb was small and I didn't think I'd have much difficulty with currents or tide rips. In a straight line, Point Ellis lay only six miles away. With luck, I could reach it in a couple hours.

The deciding factor was that I didn't feel like paddling any further than necessary. Praying for the calm weather to hold, I turned and headed directly for the point. On this shorter route, I'd be two or three miles offshore. The danger here was that if a southeast wind came up, blowing out of Tebenkof Bay, I'd have a hard time fighting my way to the beach, and could be blown right out to the middle of Chatham Strait.

Point Ellis juts way out and catches a lot of weather. As I approached, a breeze was building from the south and a mild swell accompanied it. Rocks and extensive kelp patches spread from the point to the northwest. Wanting no offshore detours, now that I'd regained close proximity to land, I worked my way through the kelp and around the point.

I followed the shoreline into Bay of Pillars and, as soon as I found a good landing spot, beached. I'd have it made now, no more big waters in a small boat for me. From here on it would be comparatively safe going. In celebration, I opened my can of peaches and slowly savored them. When done, I flattened the can with a rock and tossed it in the water. Then I launched and continued on.

The rotted remains of an abandoned cannery appeared on my right. Not much remained besides broken pilings and collapsed buildings so I didn't stop. The tide was with me now and I was making good time. Skirting rocks and tiny islands I approached a narrow channel that I assumed led to a back bay. And was suddenly apprehensive about running into Ray again.

What if he was back here and I paddled right up to

him? What would I say? Fancy meeting you again, and oh, by the way, did you cut off my anchor and pour water in my gas, causing me to lose my boat and nearly drown? Why don't you hand me that rifle and we'll talk about it? As I mulled it over, under the present circumstances, I was unable to conceive of any positive outcomes of another encounter with him. Fortunately, I didn't have long to dwell on it.

Entering the channel, the current picked up speed and I was soon hurtling through the narrows like a kayaker going down a river. I had my hands full, and it took all my concentration just keeping upright and pointed in the proper direction. The bow hit some turbulence and slewed around to starboard, nearly tossing me out. More by luck than anything else, I managed to stay aboard and get straightened out. I had a quick understanding of the thrill that Heather must get running rapids, and then it was over. The channel widened and the current spit me out into the calm expanse of a broad bay.

After taking a few minutes to regain my composure, I resumed paddling towards the head of the bay, a couple miles distant. Looking ahead, something seemed to be amiss. But it didn't have anything to do with Ray, of that I was certain. The place appeared to be all torn up. As I got closer, I realized I was looking at a logging road. It came in along my left and disappeared beyond the end of the bay. After existing in an essentially undisturbed wilderness for the last week, it came as something of a shock. Well, shocking or not, if it went the right direction, it would definitely make my portage easier.

I clambered up the steep rubble beside the shoulder of the road and looked around. The road appeared to have been built recently, but I didn't hear the sounds of any nearby machinery. Pulling on the bow line, I dragged the ding-yak up beside me, then rolled the sail cloth into a tight bundle around my meager supplies. I lashed the bundle together and tied on my plastic jugs, the grate, and my paddle. With the boat gunwale hooked on my right shoulder, and my makeshift pack under my left arm, I set off down the road, in what seemed like the right direction.

A quarter of a mile and two rest stops later I was surprised to see someone step out of the woods a short distance ahead. He was a tall, fit looking young man, decked out with a small pack and surveying instruments. I sat my awkward load down and waited. As he approached I noticed a quizzical look cross his face.

"Say," I began. "Where's this road go?"

"The way you're heading, it goes to Port Camden."

"Port Camden. And that comes out at the north end of Rocky Pass, right?"

"Right"

"Good. That's what I thought. How far is it?"

"Not far at all, just a little ways past that next corner."

"Well, that'll be easy enough." I bent to pick up the ding-yak.

"Where'ya coming from?" He asked.

"Tebenkof Bay. What about you?"

"Oh, we're laying out some new Forest Service roads, leading south of here. You'll see the flagging ahead."

Once again, I leaned over to pick up my load.

"You're sure travelling light," he said. "Been out long?"

I supposed I looked pretty worn and ragged. I could tell he was curious about me and wanted to talk. Not wanting to relate the story of losing my boat and all that, I decided to humor him.

"A while. But I like to travel light. You can buy so

much fancy camping stuff now days you might as well just stay home if you need all those comforts. I like to go out with only the basics, live off the land and scavenge what I can use off the beach."

That seemed to impress him. "Well," he said, with the hint of a grin. "I was just about to have some lunch. I wouldn't want to ruin your primitive experience, but I'd be glad to share, if you like."

I felt a smile spread across my face. "I'm no purist. As I said, I like to take advantage of whatever turns up."

He shrugged off his pack, and we sat down on a nearby log. Withdrawing the lunch, he handed me a roast beef sandwich and a hard boiled egg. I wasted no time on further talk, and eagerly tore into the food. Just as I was finishing, I noticed another surveyor break out of the woods, back towards Bay of Pillars, and start down the road towards us. I rose to my feet.

"Guess I better get going now."

My benefactor broke a Snickers candy bar in two and handed me half.

"Thanks," I said, sticking the candy bar in my pocket. I shouldered my boat and grabbed my bundle, complete with its dangling jugs and fire grate, and headed off, undoubtedly looking like some sort of wilderness, waterborne hobo.

As I rounded the corner, I heard a voice behind me.

"Who was that you were talking to, Don?"

"Just some guy passing through."

"What was he doing out here?"

"I don't know. He said he was out camping, but he looked more like a refugee from some disaster to me."

"Well," replied the other, older-sounding voice.

"You don't meet that many people wandering around out in the bush, but when you do, you never know what you'll run into."

Overhearing that conversation as I labored down the road, I couldn't help smiling to myself. After a short distance, with Port Camden in sight, I sat down and enjoyed my candy bar. From the head of this bay I knew it couldn't be far by land to Three Mile Arm. But from where I sat beside the road, a glimpse of the terrain in that direction quickly convinced me that it was too rugged to attempt. I'd have to go around.

I'd gotten an early start today and had already covered a considerable distance. Although I was tired enough to stop, I didn't want to camp by the road. As I made my way to the water's edge, I noticed several piles of fresh bear scat. A good-sized salmon stream entered Port Camden near here and bear sign was much too plentiful for me to feel comfortable about camping in the vicinity.

Wearily, I launched and resumed paddling. At least I'd remain in sheltered waters, and anything less than a brisk headwind should offer no problems. Under lowering skies, I passed two or three miles of thickly wooded, dark, somber-looking shoreline before I approached a small point of land that looked slightly more inviting.

Compared to my previous campsites, this one had little readily available firewood, and the whole area had more of a closed in, gloomy feeling about it than Chatham Strait and Tebenkof Bay had, not to mention more bugs. But there was no fresh bear sign on the point, and I reminded myself of how glad I'd been this morning to escape those big waters. I found an old snag lying on the beach and, hacking off several limbs, managed to get a fire going.

Despite having towed a lure a good portion of the

day, and having passed numerous jumping salmon, I'd failed to catch one, so settled for plain rice for dinner. It was lucky for me that guy had shared his lunch, and remembering our conversation and the one I'd overheard as I was leaving amused me, and put me in a good mood.

I awoke during the night to the sound of rain falling on my sailcloth tent. I managed to get back to sleep for a while but, soon enough, water seeping under the edge chilled me and I woke up damp on one side. Hunched up in the driest corner, I sat waiting for dawn. Considering how short Alaskan summer nights are, it seemed to take a long time for the weak light to slowly ooze into the dripping forest.

Though cold, I didn't feel like bothering with a fire this morning. Once I could see well enough to get around without risking injury, I struck camp and headed out. Paddling on the still, gray water in a steady rain was dismal, but at least it wasn't life threatening. I started out quickly to warm up, then slowed to a moderate, but steady pace. After about a half hour of using the double paddle my shoulders would begin to ache, so I'd switch to a single and paddle on one side then the other until I tired of that, then I'd switch back to the double again.

I had no idea Port Camden would be so long. It seemed to stretch on for ever. A steady trickle of water ran down the back of my neck, and before long I was pretty much soaked all over. Despite being wet and miserable, I managed to stay warm as long as I kept paddling. Finally, I reached the point where Port Camden widened out and joined Keku Strait, which led to Rocky Pass. The point held a good supply of driftwood, so I beached and, using most of my remaining gasoline, soon had a blazing fire.

I brewed a pot of tea and, as soon as the pan was cool enough, stood by the fire, sipping tea and eating my last food bar. My total remaining provisions now consisted of a handful of rice and two tea bags. As I debated whether I should make camp and stay here or move on, the sky began to lighten and the rain eased off, which helped me decide. I didn't really feel like sitting here all day, so figuring the sooner I got going, the sooner I'd get to Mac's, I shoved off.

After covering two or three more miles, whatever nourishment I'd gained from my skimpy meal had evaporated, and I found myself seriously hungry. Knowing I couldn't easily get far on my remaining energy, I decided it was time to do some fishing. An offshore reef surrounded by kelp, which marked the beginning of Rocky Pass, looked like a likely place to jig up a bottom fish.

Drifting just off the rocks, I was in the process of tying a jig to my line when I heard the sound of an approaching vessel. I looked up and saw one coming from the north. Since I was right out in the channel, there was no way he could pass by without noticing me. Shivering in the light rain, or maybe in anticipation of the encounter, I sat and waited. As the distance between us narrowed, the boat looked vaguely familiar, but I couldn't place it until he was almost up to me. It was Carl Nelson's boat, the *Edwin R.*, the boat we'd tied alongside in Cook's Cove while getting Mac's engine parts.

He slowed down as he approached, probably to avoid swamping what would appear from his wheelhouse window to be some fool sitting in a minuscule craft in the middle of the channel. I raised a hand in greeting. He hit reverse and came to a smooth halt beside me. Sliding open the pilothouse door, he stepped out on deck and looked down at me. "Anything I can do for you?"

"Maybe. You remember me? We met when I came over with Mac to get those engine parts."

"Oh yeah. Dave isn't it? You had that nice little sailboat."

"That's right."

"Well, what're you doin' sitting out here in the rain, waving at boats?"

"That's a long story. Maybe you could give me a lift while I tell ya."

"Be glad to. Come on aboard."

I paddled alongside and tossed him my bow line. "Now, if I can just get out of this thing without falling in."

Fortunately, he had a low back deck. Carl held the line while I grabbed a rail, stood up, and swung aboard. We slid the ding-yak up behind me. We'd been slowly drifting towards the rocks and Carl now dashed to the wheelhouse and put the boat in gear. He turned to me as I followed him inside.

"So, where ya headin'."

"Mac's floathouse in Three Mile Arm."

"Good. That'll be no problem. I can swing by there on my way to the Cove." Carl pushed the throttle ahead to cruising speed, then indicated the oil stove behind us with a nod of his head. "Coffee's on the stove. Help yourself while I maneuver us through this rock pile."

I hung my dripping coat and hat on hooks beside the stove and poured myself a cup of coffee. It felt great to be on a real boat again. Holding the steaming cup in both hands, I joined Carl beside the helm. He stood behind the wheel, steering us down the narrow channel between rocks and small islands.

"Is that where your sailboat is then, down at Mac's place?"

"Ah, no. It's over in Table Bay."

He looked at me in alarm. "That's no place to leave a boat. We better head right over there and get it."

"It's a little late for that," I said.

He looked at me again to make sure I wasn't joking, then thought it over for a few seconds. " Say, you weren't over there in that blow we had a few days back, were you?"

"Yeah, I was."

"Is there anything left to salvage?"

"Not unless you're interested in toothpicks."

He let that sink in for a few more seconds. "Well, if you just paddled that little canoe all the way up here from Table Bay, you must have worked up a pretty good appetite. There's bacon and eggs, and bread and whatnot in the galley. Help yourself to whatever you can find. And go ahead and dry off. There's towels in the locker by the sink and spare clothes under that bunk." He glanced at me again. "I'm not sure if they'll fit you though."

I tossed several slices of bacon in the pan, then stripped off my wet shirt and toweled off. Outweighing Carl by probably forty pounds, I figured I'd be lucky to find something to wear. I came up with an old, hooded sweatshirt and squeezed into it. My pants could just dry while I wore them. When the bacon was done, I poured out some grease and, breaking six eggs into the pan, quickly scrambled them. Carrying my plate of food, I rejoined Carl in the pilothouse and, perched on a stool in the corner, watched him navigate through the narrow pass.

The flood tide rushes into the pass from both ends and meets roughly in the middle, at a place called the Summit. Timing his trip to take advantage of the current, and to assure that there would be enough water to make it over the shallows, we had reached the Summit at high slack. Now we were heading out the other end with the ebb tide.

This, of course, is the quickest way to do it. But now, traveling with the ebb tide, came the dangerous part.

Picking up speed with the outgoing current, not only would it be harder to stop or back up if we made a wrong turn, but if we did hit a rock and got stuck, the falling tide would leave us stranded, maybe perched precariously fifteen feet above the water, with the chance of the boat toppling over.

At one time the Coast Guard had about forty buoys and markers through here, indicating various submerged reefs, rocks and tricky turns. I'd gone through once back then and found it difficult enough with the markers. Apparently though, Carl had the channel memorized. He didn't slow down, but steered calmly on.

At a particularly tight turn, appropriately called Devil's Elbow, I watched with apprehension as the fathometer indicated a depth of less than ten feet. Carl grinned as we turned and slipped past a rock just a few feet off our starboard side. "That place gets pretty skinny," he said.

"I'll say. You must know this channel pretty well. I wouldn't dream of bringing my boat through here unless they put the markers back in."

"Yeah, isn't that something. The Coast Guard roams all over now, boarding boats. Young punks in uniforms, bristling with weapons, climb aboard, sniffing ashtrays for signs of marijuana, and looking at your toilet to make sure it doesn't discharge overboard. And then they say they can't afford to maintain aids to navigation in Rocky Pass. It makes a guy wonder."

"Yeah, I know what you mean."

"I don't know," continued Carl. "It used to seem like the government was on the people's side. Now all they seem to do is bother us."

This was a common enough topic of conversation with fishermen, and Alaskans in general, and I'd held up my end of it many times before. But right now I didn't have the energy for it. Or maybe I was just too grateful to be warm and dry and well fed to complain about anything, even the government. Attempting to think of an appropriate reply, I looked back out the window. A little ripple caught my eye. "Hey. Is that a rock dead ahead?"

Carl spun the wheel and we dodged past it. "Guess I better pay attention to what I'm doin'."

We made it through the pass with no further excitement and, not wanting to disturb Carl's concentration, little more talk. He guided us inside Monte Carlo Island and into Three Mile arm. As we approached Mac's floathouse, I was disappointed to see that the *Hazel Belle* was not there.

A hundred yards before the floathouse, Carl shifted the idling *Edwin R.* into neutral. "Well, he's not here. Now what do you want to do?"

"I'm not sure. I was hoping he'd be here."

"You might as well come over to the Cove with me. With trolling starting back up in a couple days there's more chance of running into him there. If not, you can stay at my place until you figure out what you want to do."

"Thanks. That'd be great."

We turned and headed back out of the bay. Carl had just made a ten mile detour for me and I felt I should offer something in return. "I'd be happy to take the wheel on the way over, if you like."

"No that's OK. You look a little haggard. Maybe you should get some rest."

"I suppose I could use a nap."

As I lingered in the wheelhouse, he turned to me again. "If you don't mind my asking, what happened over there in Table Bay?"

"My daughter wants to start a kayak touring business in the area," I began. "She gave me a video camera and I was over there getting some footage for her. I got some good shots of Cape Decision on a beautiful day and worked my way up to Tebenkof." I proceeded to tell him the whole story, only omitting any mention of Anthony or Ray, or the missing anchor. I finished with a brief description of my trip up to Rocky Pass.

"That must've been quite a nightmare, hitting that rock in the dark, and ending up on the beach like that. That was quite a blow for summer. Winds hit fifty knots. You're lucky to have come out of it as good as you did."

"You're right about that."

"Odd though," he said, thinking it over, "that you would've picked up water in your gas that morning. Or had you just switched to a different tank?"

Though I hadn't, I could see what he was getting at. It would provide a logical explanation. But I couldn't see any point in involving him in my suspicions about Ray and Anthony. "Yeah, I had."

"That would explain it then. You must've got a shot of water last time you filled that tank. That happens up here sometimes, especially just after a fuel dock gets a new shipment. A little water that's settled in the bottom of their tank gets stirred up. Tough luck," he added.

"Oh well, like you said, it could've come out a lot worse."

"Yeah, you're lucky you're not feeding the crabs right now."

That about summed it up. There was nothing more to say. I went back to the galley and, reclining on the settee, was soon lulled to sleep by the comforting sound of the diesel engine throbbing steadily beneath me.

Chapter Twelve

I woke up when Carl slowed the engine at the entrance to Cook's Cove. Surveying the state float as we motored past in the dim evening light, I looked for the silhouette of the *Hazel Belle*, but didn't notice it. While Carl maneuvered us alongside his float, I lowered the bumpers, then secured the tie-up lines.

Carl shut off the engine and came out on deck. "I didn't see Mac's boat over there. You might as well come on up to the house with me."

I followed him up the ramp, along the boardwalk beside his shop, and into the house. He flipped a switch and turned on a light. "Storage batteries," he explained. "I can't see having to crank up the generator every time I need to turn on a light."

When I'd been here before, we didn't go in the house, but, walking in now, it looked just as I expected. Like his boat and shop, it was functional, reasonably neat and tidy, and lacking any unnecessary frills or adornment, definitely the home of a bachelor.

"I suppose you could use a shower and a little more grub," he said.

"I'm sure it couldn't hurt."

He led me to the bathroom. "I've got a propane, demand water heater, so it's all ready. Use all you want. Throw those clothes out and I'll toss 'em in the washer."

"OK. I'd be leery about touching these socks, though."

He laughed. "Maybe I'll use my rubber gloves."

After my shower, I noticed a new toothbrush and a disposable razor laid out beside the sink. I used them both and emerged from the bathroom feeling like a new man, and only slightly ridiculous wearing a pair of pants I couldn't button.

I followed my nose into the kitchen where Carl stood at the stove, frying a pan of potatoes and onions. Glancing up at my approach, he grinned. "Don't worry, your clothes will be dry soon."

"Thanks," I said. "You're quite a host. And that smells great. Ever think about going into the bed and breakfast business?"

"No. I'm sure this meal would scare away any tourists. I call it the Cook's Cove scramble."

I watched as he proceeded to open a can of Spam, cut the contents into bite sized pieces and dump them into the skillet with the potatoes and onions. Next, he grated some cheese, tossed it in, then broke half a dozen eggs on top and stirred the whole thing together. When it was done, he dished up two heaping portions and handed me a plate.

I didn't have any trouble polishing off my share and, apparently, Carl didn't either. For such a thin guy, he seemed to have a pretty healthy appetite.

He pushed aside his empty plate, tipped back his chair and regarded me. "What are you plannin' to do next?"

"I'm not sure. I was hoping to see Mac again."

"Won't do any good trying to raise him on the radio, but he may come by to ice up before fishing starts again. You're welcome to stay here until then if you like."

"Thanks. I'd like that."

"Well, I've had a long day. I'm gonna turn in. There's a bottle in the cupboard above the sink, if you want a drink. And the spare bedroom's across from the bath."

He rose, slid his plate into the sink, and left.

From where I sat at the kitchen table, I had a good view out the window and across the cove to the bar and store, and the boats moored along the float over there. I got up and poured a shot of whiskey, then returned to my chair.

Slowly sipping my drink and staring out the window, every once in a while I'd catch a glimpse of someone entering or leaving the bar and making their way down the float. With the warm glow of alcohol spreading through my body, and feeling clean and safe and relaxed, I sat, contentedly watching this small slice of human activity, until the last light across the cove blinked off.

The sound of a generator starting woke me in the morning. Looking around the room, it took me a second to realize where I was. Then I remembered, and relaxed and fell back asleep. It must have been mid morning by the time I woke up for good.

I noticed my clean clothes stacked just inside the door of the bedroom and gratefully put them on and walked into the kitchen. Carl wasn't in sight, but a fresh pot of coffee was on, so I helped myself to a cup. Lingering over my coffee, I took up last night's position and sat there looking over the cove.

The drone of a circling airplane broke in on my thoughts and I watched as the floatplane glided in for a landing. As soon as I got a good look at it, a hard knot formed in my stomach. I was sure it was Anthony. Grabbing a pair of binoculars off the window sill, I focused on the Cessna as it taxied up to the airplane float. Sure enough.

Anthony got out of the plane and tied it up, then reached back inside to get a briefcase and walked away. Through the binoculars, I followed his progress as he made his way up the ramp and along the dock to the shore. Then he walked a short distance down a boardwalk to one of the nicer looking homes in the community. He was greeted at the doorway by someone I couldn't see, and let inside.

My feelings of well-being and content deserted me, and I suddenly found myself becoming mad. Forgetting my misjudgment of the weather and poor choice of anchorage, I shifted the responsibility for losing my boat, and nearly my life, from myself to him. Perhaps Ray was more directly involved, but if it wasn't for Anthony, I would never have become entangled in the affair.

The whole reason for going to Tebenkof Bay, which subsequently led to the shipwreck, had been to confirm his part in the bear killings, in order to insure that Heather wouldn't become partners with him. Now that I'd seen his plane again, I was quite sure it was him I'd observed flying in and out of Kell Bay. Since I'd lost the evidence, I couldn't prove anything, but he wouldn't know that. Instead of convincing Heather not to have anything to do with him, I'd turn it around and tell him to leave her alone.

I gulped down my coffee and hurried out the door. Passing the shop, I noticed Carl tinkering with something at his workbench. I told him I was going across the bay to talk with someone and would be back later. My camping supplies were still in the ding-yak, so I piled them on Carl's float and shoved off. Hoping Anthony wouldn't wonder where my sailboat was, I paddled to the end of the float opposite his plane and tied there. When I got to the plane he wasn't back yet, so I sat where I had a view up the dock and waited.

Feeling restless and impatient, I fidgeted, and planned what I'd say when Anthony showed up. Eventually, he came striding down the dock, looking pleased with himself. I stood in his path so he couldn't avoid me.

"Hello Dave," he said, smiling. "I'm surprised to

see you here. Heather said you'd be on your way home."

"Well, I got sidetracked. And I'm going to get right to the point. I know what you and Ray Thorp are up to with the bears. I don't want you to have anything to do with Heather."

The smile didn't leave his face. "I'm afraid I don't know what you mean, Dave."

"I think you do. And I've got proof, videos of a dead bear, Ray in the area, you in the area, and an empty cartridge."

He laughed. "I'm glad you've been having fun playing detective. But you better go back to trying to outsmart fish. They're a lot dumber than people."

"I'm serious, Anthony. I don't want you to have anything to do with Heather."

"She's a big girl now, Dave. Do us both a favor and stay out of it. Let her make up her own mind."

I could see he wasn't swayed, and decided to push it. "Either you agree to leave her out of your life, or I take my evidence to the cops."

His smile hardened as he looked at me. Then he took half a step forward and put his left arm over my shoulders, as if in a friendly gesture. As I recoiled, he slid his arm down my back and quickly patted my stomach a few times with his other hand. I pushed his hand away and stepped back.

He laughed. "No, you're not smart enough for that. You don't know what you're getting into." His smile turned into a condescending grin. "Now listen to me. I don't like being threatened. You may have scared Ray off, but that's not me. I know you don't have anything against me that would stick, but I don't like cops sniffing around. And I'll know if they start."

"Now Heather will be up here again, with or without me. You want to threaten me, well, if you want to keep your daughter safe, you better hope the cops stay away. If they get on my trail I'm gonna know who put 'em there. And I'm not gonna like it. Remember, it's a big country out here. Sometimes people can just disappear."

As Anthony turned and calmly walked to his plane, I stood open mouthed and rooted in place. For a fleeting instant I had an almost overwhelming urge to kill him, tackle him from behind, get my hands on his neck and choke the life right out of him. Maybe if I thought I actually had a chance to accomplish it before someone pulled me off, I might have tried it. Instead, I just stood there dumbly and watched him leave. I could hardly believe what had just happened.

My mind racing, and oblivious to the boats and people around me, I paced back and forth on the float. What had I done? I'd proven beyond a shadow of a doubt to myself that Anthony was a criminal. But so what? Had I really placed my daughter's life in jeopardy, or was he just a blowhard? Either way, I knew I'd never go to the cops now. I didn't have evidence anyway.

And what would Heather do if I told her of this conversation? Surely she'd resent my meddling, but would she believe me? Hard to say. I could hardly believe it, and I'd just heard it. I could easily imagine people telling me I was suffering from some sort of post trauma stress and had blown the conversation way out of proportion. Pretty soon I wouldn't believe I'd heard it either. Maybe that would be best. Would Anthony really consider carrying out a threat like that? Most likely he'd just wanted to scare me off.

Once I'd gotten myself calmed down enough, I walked into the bar. At my approach, Jim looked up from a pile of receipts.

"Jesus, Dave. What happened to you? You look like you just saw a ghost. Better have a drink." Without waiting for my reply, he poured a shot and handed it to me.

"Thanks. Maybe I could use one." I took the glass and sat down beside him. I drank slowly and didn't say anything for quite a while. Besides us, the place was empty. I finished the drink and sat the glass down.

"Care for another?"

"No thanks. But maybe you could tell me something. You know that guy that just flew out of here a little bit ago?"

"I know who he is."

"What was he doing out here?"

He looked at me for a second. "Well, I guess that's no secret. He's buying some property over on Sumner Island from old Mrs. Riley. Used to be a fox farm. They homesteaded over there for many years. Unlike most people back then, they got legal title to the place."

That was bad news. It might mean that Anthony would remain in the area. "What do you know about Anthony Richardson?"

"Not a lot. Why?"

"You see, my daughter is planning on starting a kayak touring business in the area. She was talking about going in partners with him. I don't like or trust the guy. In fact I just had a conversation with him that definitely confirmed that. The trouble is, I'm not sure what to do."

"I think you could be right about him."

"What makes you say that?"

Jim took a look around, and even though no one else was in the room, he lowered his voice when he spoke. "It's not something I would normally talk about, but since you're directly involved I suppose you have a right to know."

He paused.

"Now don't get me wrong. I'm no stool pigeon, but I have an old friend, a State Trooper. He's pretty high up in rank by now. Sometimes he asks me to keep my eyes and ears open about a certain person. Then, if I have a little trouble with serving a minor or something, he puts in a good word for me. It's no big deal, that's just the way life works."

"Right."

"I just got this place out here, you know, and was working in Wrangell previously. I've owned and worked in a lot of taverns in the state and my friend and I go back a long ways. He knows he can trust me to keep my mouth shut, so he fills me in with a little background on a person sometimes."

Jim paused, and glanced around the bar again. Seeing no one, he continued. "Well, last winter my friend called me. Anthony had just moved to Wrangell and they were interested in him. Seems there had been a big-time smuggling and poaching ring operating in the Anchorage area, bringing drugs into villages and smuggling out illegal animal parts. They handled everything from polar bear skins to walrus tusks to falcon chicks. And branched out into guiding illegal trophy hunts, and supplying stuffed animals to collectors. The more rare and expensive, the better."

"The state and the feds were working together on a sting operation. They'd infiltrated the ring and were about to close in when something went wrong. Their agent went on a buying trip and never came back. Shortly after that a potential key witness also disappeared. The case fell apart. They hauled a few guys in for questioning, but, without the bodies, it's hard to prove anything. They thought Anthony might know something about it."

My throat went dry and my guts clenched. My worst fears about Anthony had suddenly been not only confirmed, but exceeded. He was a real criminal. Then it dawned on me. That strange business of him touching me had been a search for a hidden tape recorder. When he'd confirmed that I didn't have one, he'd laughed, then made his threat. He was right, I didn't know what I was getting into. I should have stuck with fish.

Two fishermen sauntered into the bar and Jim excused himself. When his customers left with a case of beer and a bottle, he returned to my side.

"You OK? I hope I didn't upset you with that information. Anthony may or may not have been involved, but I figured I ought to let you know."

"Yeah, I'm OK. And I appreciate you telling me. Thanks." I rose to my feet. "I'll see you later."

My head spinning, I walked woodenly out the door and onto the float. What could I do now? Sure, I could go to the authorities with my story and they'd be interested, but what good would that do? They couldn't even protect their own agent. How could I expect them to protect my daughter? There was only one thing to do. I'd have to take care of things myself. I'd go into Wrangell and find Anthony and have it out with him, settle things one way or another. Striding purposefully down the float, with my head in a blur, I almost ran into Mac.

"Whoa there," he said. "Where you going in such a rush? I saw your dinghy back there but where's your sailboat?"

"That's a long story, and I'll tell you later. Right now I've got to go to Wrangell and take care of some business." I started to step around him.

"Hold on there a minute. How you gonna get there? If you plan on paddling that contraption into Wrangell, a few minutes one way or another won't make any difference. Come on over to the boat." Grasping my elbow, he steered me to the *Hazel Belle.*

We made our way down into the foc'sle, and he sat me at the galley table. "Had anything for lunch yet? I can smell you've already had a drink."

"No, I haven't eaten."

"Good. Just so happens I just got in and still have a pot of soup on the stove."

He filled a bowl and set it and a slice of buttered bread in front of me. It smelled good and I automatically started eating. As my whirling mind slowed down, I realized all I'd consumed so far today had been coffee and alcohol, which wasn't helping my mental stability. I began to relax. Mac joined me in a bowl, and I had seconds. I sat for a long while without speaking. Finally Mac said, "Now what's this about a long story?"

He listened calmly as I told my tale, beginning with when I'd left Cook's Cove and encountered Ray at Kell Bay. I included all of the details and, when I got to the part about camping out and paddling up Chatham Strait and through Gedney Harbor, I saw Mac smiling. "What's so funny?" I said.

"Just remembering how you told me about wanting to, ah, how was it, get closer to nature this summer, feel the breeze in your face, get in touch with the land. Sounds like you got your wish."

I couldn't help but grin. "Well, you're right there. I got all of that I wanted. The trouble is, in the process, I got more than I bargained for."

Mac listened impassively as I continued with my story. But, when I got to the part about Anthony saying that if I wanted to keep Heather safe I'd better hope the cops didn't come snooping around, a change came over him. His head jerked around and I saw that intense flash in his eyes.

"He said that?"

"Yes, he said that. And furthermore, I'm afraid he means it." I proceeded to tell Mac what Jim had just told me. "And now you know why I'm so worried," I concluded.

"What was that guy doing out here? Did Jim say?"

"Yeah, I guess he just bought some land over on Sumner Island from somebody here."

At this news, Mac seemed to relax. He leaned back and rubbed the stubble on his chin. "Well, I wouldn't worry so much about it. He's probably just shooting off his mouth."

"I might have believed that before I listened to Jim, but now I don't know. I don't feel like I can just ignore it."

"What were you planning on doing? Going into town to call him out for a duel in the street?"

"I don't know," I admitted lamely.

"Listen," said Mac. "There's nothing for you to do now. If you go in there you could just get yourself in trouble. Heather's off in college for the winter. She won't be up here before next summer, so there's nothing to worry about. You should just forget about it and head on home now."

"I don't know. It's not that easy to just forget. I feel like I should settle it now and get it over with."

"I know how you feel, but think about it. You're not likely to accomplish anything besides just digging yourself in deeper. Which you seem pretty good at doing."

"You might be right."

"I know I'm right. Do something useful and go home and check in with your wife. She's probably worried about you. Now come on." He led me off the boat and back into the bar.

"Hey Jim," he hollered, as we entered. "Is the mail plane from Ketchikan due in this afternoon?"

Jim looked up in surprise. "Yup, sure is."

"Good, call 'em up and book a flight out of here on it for Dave."

I began to protest. "I don't even have any money, since I lost my wallet."

"Yes you do." Mac grinned. "I think you accidently misplaced this." He handed me the same wad of bills I'd stuck back in his money jar after we'd been fishing.

"What's it gonna be?" Asked Jim.

"Call 'em up," I said. "I think Mac's smarter than I am."

We had an hour before the plane would arrive. I paddled over to Carl's and thanked him for his hospitality. Then I stashed the ding-yak and my stuff behind Jim's house. I told him I'd pick them up next season. Doing something had helped take my mind off my worries, but as we stood waiting for the plane to unload, I began to have second thoughts about flying away.

"I don't know," I said to Mac. "I wonder if this is really the best thing to do. I hate leaving things hanging over my head like this."

"I know what you mean," he said, ushering me toward the plane. "But try not to worry." Just before I stepped aboard, he placed a hand on my shoulder. "Just remember, a lot of things can happen between now and next summer."

Chapter Thirteen

With a roar, the floatplane accelerated across the cove and lifted off. The pilot banked the plane to the right and we rose over the strait, quickly leaving the village behind. It had been an abrupt departure and I was having difficulty adjusting to the idea that I was suddenly on my way home. Before I knew it, we were descending into Ketchikan. I got out of the plane feeling slightly disoriented.

In order to slow things down and give myself time to adjust, I considered taking the ferry south from here. But I learned that the boat wouldn't depart for two more days, and didn't feel like waiting that long. A southbound jet would leave in less than an hour, and I had just enough money on me to buy a ticket. Soon, I was airborne again, rushing homeward over the B.C. coast.

A balmy summer evening greeted me as I jockeyed through the crowds and stepped out of the Sea-Tac Airport terminal. I tucked my jacket under my arm, unbuttoned my shirt and rolled up the sleeves. After a short wait, I was speeding along the freeway in a commuter bus to downtown Seattle.

I'd grown up in a rural part of the state and had never felt comfortable in the city. But now, coming so directly from the bush to the bright lights, the difference was so radical that instead of the city grating on me as usual, I found myself marvelling at it all. The events of the previous week began to recede to a distant corner of my brain.

From a phone booth downtown, I dialed my wife's number.

"Hello, Karen."

"Why Dave, I was just thinking about you. Where are you? We sure got a good phone connection."

"That's because I'm in Seattle."

"You are? Really?"

"Yeah, really. Here, you can listen to the traffic." I held the phone out towards the drone of the passing cars.

"All right, I believe you. But how did you get back so soon?"

"That's kind of a long story. I'd be happy to tell you over dinner. Know of any good restaurants?"

"Not really, but I'm sure we could find one. Where are you?"

"Corner of 4th and Union"

"OK. Wait right there. I'll pick you up. It'll take about fifteen minutes."

I saw her blue Honda coming, and when she stopped at the light, I rushed out and climbed into the passenger seat. She gave me a quick kiss.

"Dave, this is such a surprise."

"I know, it's a surprise for me too."

The light changed and we surged ahead with the traffic. "What do you want to eat?" She asked.

"I don't care, anything's fine."

"There's a nice Italian restaurant near the apartment. We might as well go there."

As soon as we parked and got out, I gave her a big hug and another kiss. I was struck by how much she resembled Heather. Like one of those old TV commercials, they could just about pass for sisters instead of mother and daughter. "You look great," I said. "Being around all those college kids must be good for you."

"Oh Dave, it just makes me feel old. But you look healthy. I think you may have lost a little weight."

"That's possible. I did skip a few meals recently."

We ordered and had a glass of wine while waiting for our food. "Did you see Heather and Dwight when they came back?" I asked.

"Yes, briefly. They said they had a marvelous time. And Dwight seemed pretty impressed by your friend Mac."

"What do you think of Dwight?"

"He seems like a nice, sincere young man. What about you?"

"Yeah, he seemed fine, a little naive maybe, but nice enough. Did they tell you about the bear chase?"

"Yes. I think that was quite an adventure for Dwight."

Recalling him thrashing around in the brush, I grinned. "I'm sure it was. Do you think he and Heather are serious about one another?"

"They're serious enough for now, but I wouldn't be surprised if they eventually went their separate ways."

The waitress brought our plates and I dug in. We ate, interrupting our dinner occasionally with idle chatter and bits of small talk. Halfway through the meal, I noticed Karen studying me.

"Dave, I'm still waiting to hear why you got back so soon. And where's your boat?"

"Well, I flew back. And the boat's in splinters, up in Chatham Strait."

"You're sure acting casual about it. What happened?"

"I chose a bad anchorage and a storm came up. I lost the boat on the rocks."

"Then what happened? Were you in danger?"

"Oh, briefly. But I salvaged the dinghy, so when it calmed down I paddled out of there. Then a guy picked me up and gave me a ride."

"Isn't that the same area where Heather wants to lead kayak tours? If a storm wrecked your sailboat, what would happen to them in little kayaks?"

"They'd be fine. They don't have to anchor out. Camping on the beach, they'd wait out the storm, safe and sound, then be on their way. If I had been in a kayak, I'd have had no problem."

"That makes me feel better, but that's terrible about you losing your boat after all the work you did. Don't you feel awful?"

"Not really. You know, I realized something while I was out there. That boat was nice and I enjoyed building it, but it didn't really matter that much to me. I was just using it to escape. It's not that important. It's not nearly as important as us getting back together."

Karen's eyes misted over and she dabbed at them with a napkin. She didn't say anything, but reached across the table and took my hand.

Later that evening I called Heather. She was surprised to hear where I was calling from, but I thought I detected a note of happiness in her voice when I told her. When I explained how I'd come to be there, she consoled me over the loss of my boat. I apologized for losing her camera and told her I'd replace it. She seemed enthusiastic about her trip and the future possibilities of the business, and, though he loomed large in my mind, I carefully avoided any mention of Anthony. I didn't tell Heather, but I was following her advice. I'd take care of my own relationships before I tried to tell her how to handle her own.

I stayed with Karen in her apartment for several

days. Between her part-time job and attending classes at the University, she had a busy schedule. I helped out with cooking and little household chores but, other than that, didn't have much to do. We got along well and enjoyed each other, but soon I grew restless. I began to understand why she had needed a change.

After dinner on Friday evening, while Karen tried to study, I flicked through the TV channels then turned the set off in disgust. "What about going out to a movie tonight?"

"I'd love to, Dave, but the end of the quarter is coming up and I really need to do this."

I paced around the apartment for awhile, then opened a curtain and stood looking out the window. Unless you like parking lots, and streets and buildings, it wasn't much of a view.

Karen laid her book aside. "What are you doing?"

"Looking out the window. Why?"

"I'm having a hard time concentrating with you pacing around like a caged lion."

"Sorry."

"I think you need something to do."

"You're right." I walked over and sat down beside her. "And I've been thinking. It's still August. I feel guilty about showing up only to leave again, but I'm thinking about making a fishing trip."

"Isn't it late for going back to Alaska?"

"I'm thinking about going off the coast for albacore."

She pondered that for a moment. "I think that's a good idea. You haven't done it recently, but you said you enjoyed it."

She was right. For the last few years I'd fished

salmon right up to the end and had finished up way out by Yakutat, in the Gulf of Alaska. By the time I'd gotten back from there, I'd had enough and hung it up for the season. In previous years, though, sometimes I'd quit salmon early and made a few tuna trips. Like all fishing, sometimes it had paid off and other times it hadn't.

I'd saved enough money over the years to be able to afford to take a season off. Originally that had been my intention, to take one whole season off. But since my sailing trip had been cut short, and my troller was ready, and Karen was busy, I might as well go. A little more income certainly couldn't hurt.

Sunday morning we boarded the ferry for the trip across Puget sound, then drove for an hour and a half to our home on the outskirts of Port Angeles. Situated on five acres in the foothills of the Olympic Mountains, with a view overlooking the Straits of Juan de Fuca, it was a nice enough place, but seemed empty and barren now and neither of us felt like spending much time there. Making a quick inspection, I determined that everything was in order. Then I packed a bag with clothes and we drove down to the boat harbor.

In the off season, my boat, a 47 foot fiberglass model, built by a popular northwest yard, blended in with the rest of the fleet crowded along the float. Now, the *Pacific Star* looked lonely at the nearly deserted dock. We carried my stuff down and climbed aboard.

In our first years of marriage, Karen had fished with me some, but it hadn't worked out too well and, as soon as she became pregnant, she'd happily stayed behind. Since then she hadn't taken much interest in my boats and rarely came aboard. Now she busied herself inventorying the cupboards.

I'd owned the *Pacific Star* for ten years and had spent a considerable amount of time aboard. She was like a second home to me and, even though I'd been glad to not be fishing this spring, I was happy to be back aboard now. I started the engine to charge the batteries, and turned on the refrigerator.

Karen and I spent the afternoon shopping and stocked the boat with a supply of food. When trolling for albacore tuna, depending on the weather, you can spend days, even weeks at a time offshore, and it's a good idea to have plenty of everything.

We had dinner at a cafe in town, then Karen dropped me off at the dock and headed back for Seattle. I spent the evening going over my gear. I was excited about the prospect of going fishing, but wondered if I was merely escaping again. In the end, I decided I wasn't. It was fishing season and I was just following my chosen occupation.

Albacore migrate past Washington late each summer, but seldom come close to shore. Typically they pass a hundred or more miles off. Unlike in salmon fishing, the fish are spread out over such a vast extent of open ocean that fishermen tend to be cooperative about passing on information as to their location and catches. By listening on my radios and talking with one of the local boats who was out on the grounds, I developed an idea of where to head.

Ten hours of solid running after passing Cape Flattery, then I slowed to six knots and put out my gear. The first day's fishing was poor and I only caught seventeen fish. The beauty of albacore fishing is that it tends to be an uncrowded, noncompetitive fishery. The drawback is that you can steam all over the ocean burning hundreds of gallons of fuel, possibly in rough conditions, and catch very little.

I drifted at night and trolled in a southwesterly direction during the day. The second day was only a little better, but the third day I spotted a few boats on the horizon and began catching more fish. The weather remained decent and the fishing improved. For several days I enjoyed steady fishing, catching around a hundred fish per day.

I'd been on the grounds eight days when the radio reported a weather system approaching. The fish had scattered and I wasn't catching much when I heard the report, so I didn't hesitate to pull my gear and head in. Using the marine operator, I called Karen and she agreed to take a few days off and meet me in Astoria, Oregon.

A sixteen hour run brought me to the mouth of the Columbia River. In rising wind and swells, I jogged for a few hours ten miles off the river mouth, waiting for daylight and the flood tide before crossing the bar.

Finished with unloading the catch, I took a shower and was catching up on my sleep, when Karen found me at the dock. We drove south along the coast, and rented a motel room for two nights. The weather was lousy and many tourists complained, but we didn't mind. Walking the windy beach, browsing through the shops and eating out, we had great time. It reminded me of a second honeymoon. On the ride back to Astoria I thought about the future.

"What do you want to do this winter, Karen?" I asked.

"It might not make a lot of sense to you, but I want to get my degree. It's just something I want to complete. After that, I'm not sure."

"How long will that take?"

"At the rate I'm going, two more quarters. If I quit my job and take more classes, one."

"Good. I think you should quit and take the classes. Here's my idea. I'll make another trip or two, then moor the boat at Fisherman's Terminal in Seattle for the winter. I want to upgrade the freezer system so that'll give me something to do this fall. I'll move in with you and work on the boat during the day. If you get tired of me I can always stay on the boat. Then, when you finish with school, we'll take off on a vacation. Where would you like to go?"

"Gee, I'm not sure."

"Well, you can think about it. Maybe we can visit Heather around Christmas time, go skiing together or something, and take off from there."

"Dave, I can hardly believe you said that. We tried for years to get you to go skiing with us and all we got was wisecracks about space boots and tight fitting costumes."

She was right, but I didn't reply.

Several miles later she said. "You know, I've always wanted to see New Orleans."

My next trip didn't work out so well. The weather had calmed and I headed out the day after Karen dropped me off. I ran west and had gotten in only three days of mediocre fishing when another weather system was reported to be on the way. I hated to go back in so soon but the comments on the radio from the boats two and three hundred miles off convinced me that the weather was serious enough to warrant running in. If I was out where they were I'd just have to tough it out, but since I was only a hundred and twenty miles off Westport I might as well run for it.

The storm chased me in, and I was glad enough to be there. Numerous other tuna boats had ended up in Westport and I spent four days resting, eating, and exchanging sea stories with the other fishermen, and catching up on oil changes and boat maintenance. I felt good about things in general and the direction my life was now taking in particular, except for one thing.

Sometimes, when I laid down at night, just before drifting off, Anthony's comments would come back to haunt me. Then my feelings of well-being would desert me. And no matter how the thoughts churned and twisted through my mind, I could think of nothing to do other than what I was now doing, though it didn't seem like enough.

By putting my own life in order, hopefully I'd gain credibility in Heather's eyes, but then what? If she believed me about Anthony and suddenly agreed to have nothing to do with him, he'd suspect me, of course, not that I cared about that. But what about when he noticed the cops taking an interest in him, as they inevitably would sooner or later? What would happen then? Could I ask Heather to not go back to Alaska at all? Even if she agreed to not go into partnership with him, I doubted she'd take the threat seriously enough for that. But from what Jim had told me, and the way Anthony had searched me for a recorder and then laughed, I took him seriously.

I longed to talk it over with Karen, but that was out of the question. Things were now going well between us, better than ever, and I didn't want to burden her with the mess I'd caused. For now it was my own private torment and I'd have to bear it alone.

When the weather broke, I headed out again. Ninety miles off, I came to the warmer water which albacore prefer. I put out my gear and began trolling in a northwesterly direction, prospecting for fish. For three days I didn't find much. Radio reports indicated good fishing two hundred and fifty miles off Newport Oregon, but that was too far away to get excited over. Sometimes concentrations of albacore show up off Vancouver Island in September, so I kept heading north, picking up a few fish along the way.

Luck was with me, and on my sixth day out I encountered heavy fishing just eighty miles off Vancouver Island. Conditions were excellent and, so far, only a small fleet was working the area; just enough boats to keep track of the rapidly moving and schooling fish. I pulled 15 lb. tuna aboard as fast as I was able to and on some days had to quit early so my freezer system could keep up. It was just as well. By then I was totally exhausted anyway.

For a week the calm weather held and fishing ranged anywhere from good to excellent. Several large boats in the area with better freezers and a crew of two or three men racked up some impressive scores. I was more than happy with my catch, and when the schools dissipated, gratefully headed for home with nearly ten tons of frozen tuna aboard.

I unloaded in Port Angeles and briefly considered making another trip. But, by the time I was rested up and ready to go again, radio reports indicated that the action had tapered off and the weather was worsening. Soon enough it would be time for an equinox storm and I didn't relish the idea of running for two solid days to get out to the fish, only to have to run back or get thrashed in a storm. Earlier in my life, hoping to get another big load, I might have gone for it. Now, having already made much more than I expected to this season, I was happy to quit while ahead. Instead of pointing the bow seaward, I aimed for Seattle.

Karen met me at the dock when I pulled into Fisherman's Terminal. It felt strange tying up there, but I would soon get used to it. Fortunately, when the traffic was light, her apartment was only ten or fifteen minutes away so, if I timed it right, the commute wouldn't be bad.

Concentrating on school, Karen had quit her job and would graduate this quarter. She also gave notice that we'd vacate the apartment in December. Arrangements had been made to spend Christmas in Montana with Heather. She found a cabin just out of Missoula for us and we reserved it for ten days. After that, we'd head for New Orleans. With the exception of occasionally being haunted by thoughts of Anthony, I couldn't have been happier.

The letter came in November. In order to beat the rush hour, I'd left the boat early and arrived home before Karen. Looking through the day's mail, I noticed an envelope for me, sent to our Port Angeles address and postmarked from Alaska. It had been forwarded here and bore no return address. Mystified, I opened the letter.

The envelope contained a single copy of an article which had been torn from a page of the Ketchikan newspaper. Having no idea what it was about, but fearing the worst, I quickly scanned through it, then sat and read it carefully once more.

The article stated the search for a missing person from Wrangell, Anthony J. Richardson, had been called off. When reported overdue, authorities had located his floatplane at the property he'd recently purchased on Sumner Island, but had been unable to find any trace of him. It was feared that he might have fallen in and drowned but divers were unable to locate his body. Search efforts were called off due to poor weather and a lack of leads. Scrawled across the bottom of the page were the words. "Like the man said, it's a big country out here and sometimes people just disappear."

I read the article once more, then slid it and the envelope into the bottom of the trash. I wondered what had happened exactly, but knew I'd never ask.

The End